With the isolation, mystery and power of the mountains as a back drop, Durango, Colorado has a history rich with family legacies and traditions. A twist of fate and the power of will against will catapults a prominent Durango family into chaos and murder.

Randy Ord III, heir to the Ord mining Company fortunes is dead. Danielle Maynard Ord, the victim's wife, fostered an elaborate plot to kill him to end his abuse. Ruth Ord, the victim's sister, tired of parental favoritism to the exclusion of her contributions to the family also had a motive to want him dead. Beatrice Ord, mother of Randy and Ruth, was used to manipulating and controlling as the matriarch of the Ord dynasty. She dogs her rebellious son, rides her subservient daughter and attempts to buy Danielle and Randy's child after he is murdered so that the child will become the new heir to the Ord fortunes.

It is up to detective Sandy March to sift through the lines of this dysfunctional family and the abused wife and ferret out the real killer. Trying to keep his judgment from being compromised by the growing attraction he has for one of the prime suspects, Danielle Ord

What They Are Saying About
Death By Candlelight

Billie A. Williams has breathed life into a believable set of characters you'll love or love to hate. The story is packed with enthralling plot twists that keep the reader glued to the page as the dark dynamics of relationships and crime unfold. Death by Candlelight holds rare delights in store for the murder mystery lover.

Susan J. Letham
http://www.Inspired2Write.com

Death by Candlelight portrays the unbending force upon humans to repeat generational cycles of abusers and victims. Cycles that love, faith or hope can rarely supersede. Yet, with the unraveling of a murder, we are still left with a glimmer of hope.

Shelly Moloney,
Author *Star Slurry*

DEATH BY CANDLELIGHT is a fast-paced read filled with a diverse cast of characters who each have their own motives for murder. Just when you think you've hit the calm after the storm, Williams' story takes the reader in a new and more intriguing direction.

Shirley Kawa-Jump
THE VIRGIN'S PROPOSAL,
Silhouette Romance, January 2003
Writing classes: shirleyjump-subscribe@yahoogroups.com

The story? TERRIFIC. I could hardly wait to finish it..reminds me of Sydney Sheldon....

> Judy Bozicevich,
> Administrative Assistant,
> Edward Jones Company

Every time I thought I had **Death by Candlelight** figured out, Williams threw in a new twist that left me thinking, *I DIDN'T see that coming!* **Death By Candlelight** isn't so much a "Who-Done-It" as it is a character driven story filled with more twists than a Colorado mountain road. It's a quick read without any lulls in the action. **Death by Candlelight** is a fabulous first novel by Wisconsin writer, Billie Williams. Be sure to watch her career—I'm sure we'll hear from her again—at least I hope we do!

> —Beth Erickson
> http://filbertpublishing.com

Wings

Death By Candlelight

by

Billie A. Williams

A Wings ePress, Inc.

General Fiction Mystery Novel

Wings ePress, Inc.

Edited by: Marilyn Kapp
Copy Edited by: Dianne Hamilton
Senior Editor: Marilyn Kapp
Managing Editor: Dianne Hamilton
Executive Editor: Lorraine Stephens
Cover Artist: Michelle Phelps

All rights reserved

Names, characters and incidents depicted in this book are products of the author's imagination or are used fictitiously. Any resemblance to actual events, locales, organizations, or persons, living or dead, is entirely coincidental and beyond the intent of the author or the publisher.

No part of this book may be reproduced or transmitted in any form or by any means, electronic or mechanical, including photocopying, recording, or by any information storage and retrieval system, without permission in writing from the publisher.

Wings ePress Books
http://www.wings-press.com

Copyright © 2002 by Billie A. Williams
ISBN 1-59088-901-0

Published In the United States Of America

October 2002

Wings ePress Inc.
403 Wallace Court
Richmond, KY 40475

Dedication

To my Mother
and all those people who believed in me.

One

"Bitch."

Danielle heard the profanity before she felt the blow to the back of her head, which knocked her sideways off her chair. Hot wax spilled with her, pouring across her arm and coating everything from table to floor like lava flowing from a volcano. With a brutal stroke of his arm, Randy swept the table clear of all her candles and supplies. The crash was deafening and heightened her pain. Randy didn't wait for her to recover. He grabbed her by one arm, picking her up like a pile of dirty rags. She landed with a thud against the doorframe. Pain shot up her side. She wouldn't scream. She wouldn't cry. She wouldn't give him the satisfaction. She glared at Randy.

"Next time I tell you to go get beer for my friends, you jump, understand?" Randy roared. He smashed the back of his hand across her face.

"Clean up this fucking mess and you before I get back or there will be hell to pay," he said, staggering out of the room. "You and your damn candles, that's all you think about. I'm sick of it."

The kitchen door slammed hard enough to rattle the windows. Tears streamed down her face as she lay in a heap where she had fallen. Her body throbbed with pain. The hot wax on her arm had cooled to a warm paste but the burning sensation intensified. She pulled herself into a sitting position and took stock of all the parts where she hurt. Nothing felt broken, not this time anyway. She crawled over to where the wax for her latest batch of candles puddled on the bright red and gray tiles of the craft room floor. Still in a dazed half-conscious state of mind, she began peeling and scooping wax back into the kettle and turned off the hot plate. Tears clouded her vision. *"Where have all the flowers gone . . . "* she began singing in a quiet bird-like voice.

Running out to get beer for him and his cronies disgusted her. She hoped ignoring him would work, hoped that everyone would leave and he would pass out. This latest party was running into the third day. *How long can he last?* Usually after he woke up from an extended drunk, Randy would be apologetic and doting, loving her as though he meant it. She had fallen in love with that Randy. No such luck this time, this time he seemed to gain energy from the violence against her. There was a silence when all Randy's friends left; the hollow silence, now that Randy had left too, seemed ominous. "I should have known better," she sobbed, tears spattering in the soft wax coating the floor. Outside, the Silverton Narrow Gauge Railroad Train moaned with the familiar cry like the howl of a gray wolf that searched for its mate. It echoed Danielle's pain. *"Yesterday, all my troubles seemed so far away..."* The words and music crashed through her mind flooding her thoughts with memories.

The loving relationship she once enjoyed had now turned dark and sinister. He used to be fun. Now, she no longer knew the man she was living with. He was increasingly more violent. Anything would trip his hair trigger temper and set him off. *How long will it be before he kills me?* The thought made her shudder.

Danielle knew Randy could be back in an hour if he went to the Billy Goat Saloon where all the bikers hung out or he could take off on his Harley and be gone for days. She never knew for sure when he left like this.

They had only been together a year the first time he left and she had missed him with a passion. Worried sick about him for four days, she'd tortured herself with guilt and *what ifs,* waiting for him to return. When he finally did come home, he had found her waiting for him eager to forget the fight that had caused him to slap her around. Later he apologized and said he would never do it again. She had believed him. After all, he had not really beaten her, at least not that time; he had just slapped her and shoved her down. As she thought about the accelerating violence, the time he broke her arm seemed long ago. That had scared her. He did take her to the emergency room the next day when he was sober. "Tell them you fell down the stairs," he said.

The emergency room personnel were not inclined to believe that story and she had to do some tall talking to convince them it was nothing more than a clumsy accident. Maybe that time it *was* her fault, if she hadn't made him mad, maybe that wouldn't have happened. She shouldn't have nagged him about getting a job. That time when she asked, he told her he had gone for a ride to sort things out. "What did that mean?" He told her to keep her nose out of his business. She never asked again. Now, as her body ached with pain, remembering his apologies after each new outburst of violence, she wondered if his promise to never do it again meant the beating or the running away. The answer was all too clear recently.

The day she met him he came into the Office Bar & Grill wearing faded blue jeans and a faded blue chambray work shirt. His deep brown hair and mahogany brown eyes swept her off her feet. He was her first encounter with a cowboy, Stetson hat, boots and all. She got shivers just thinking about the tall, lean cowboy with the slow drawl and easy manner. His smile caused butterflies in her stomach or perhaps lower. And it still did.

After her shower, Danielle laid across the bed to rest her aching body. She started to dream almost immediately.

She was in a dark tall house that seemed sandwiched between the other houses in a dusty coal town. Her father didn't have a job and the family was barely surviving. Sometime early in the morning, she awoke to the sound of her parents fighting again. She heard her mother scream and rushed into their bedroom. Sunlight snuck red through the cheap gauze curtains. Traffic grumbled outside on the street. Danielle heard the short agitated blasts of the coal train whistle as it rumbled along the tracks a block away. The windows rattled with its passing. She hated the train that disturbed their foundation four times a day. Its angry wail and dirty puffs of coal dust turned the snow gritty black within hours of falling pristine white. The train seemed to punctuate the black trouble of their lives here.

Father was in bed; anger and hate darkened his already black eyes. Her mother was on the floor holding the back of her head, tears streamed down her face. Her hair was disheveled, her face ashen. Clothes tossed on a chair beside the bed looked like a deflated scarecrow. The bed covers, dragged to the floor, surrounded mother's thin frame.

"Get out, get out of this room. You don't belong in here." Her father snarled at her.

"It's okay honey. Go on. I'm okay," mother said

"She'd be fine if she got her lazy ass out of bed and got some breakfast. She's nothing but a lazy bitch," her father said throwing a pillow at her mother.

"Leave her out of this," her mother retorted and then cowered as he raised a boot to throw.

She shivered with fear for her mother.

Danielle woke up sweating and hating herself for being weak like her mother. The dream was from years ago. It seemed like forever since she had last seen her parents. Things hadn't always been like that. After they moved again things got better. When her father wasn't drinking things were pretty normal. She could still see her father's brown/black eyes, how they grew intensely black when he was angry. It was such a contrast to her blue-eyed, blonde mother. They made a great couple. His drinking finally killed him at the age of fifty-five. Her mother had died a few months later. Danielle guessed her mother couldn't live without her father. Their relationship had been stormy but they always loved as passionately as they fought. She missed her mother. She needed her advice. She needed her companionship. There was no one to tell her secrets to anymore. Certainly, no one she could tell about Randy and his tirades.

Two

Randy returned three hours later.

Danielle had cleaned up the disaster he'd made out of her equipment and set the broken candles aside to be melted down and re-poured. Using some healing ointment on the burn that the hot wax had left on her arm and make up to cover the bruise on her cheek, she closed the door to her hobby room to shut out his memory of the incident. The salve on her arm made the redness of the burn glisten like a stoplight on a rainy night.

Dinner was ready to go on the table when she heard Randy's footsteps approaching the door. Silence weighted the air in the cramped apartment. He glared at her as he practically fell into the room. A vanilla candle flickered at the sudden burst of air sucked toward the door. She had deliberately lit the candle to create a mood and to eradicate the staleness of the apartment's beer, marijuana and cigarettes. She hoped if, or when, Randy returned the candle aroma would lighten his mood.

Cautiously Danielle served him pork chops, mashed potatoes with gravy and green beans then sat down to her own plate.

"You know I hate green beans," he shouted, throwing his plate across the tiny kitchen. He shoved his chair back as he stood. The chair toppled with a loud crash. He kicked it aside.

Danielle kept her eyes on her plate dreading the blow she knew would follow. Instead, she heard him clomping toward the bedroom. He reached the doorway before he started retching. Vomit blew across the bedroom floor. He avoided the mess, stumbled to the bed, and fell across it.

Danielle sat staring at her plate afraid to move. She wished he would die. Silence, then a soft snoring came from the bedroom. She knew he'd passed out and would be that way for hours. Grateful, that for now, she was safe she quietly began clearing the table, humming softly, *"Where have all the flowers gone..."*

"I can't live like this," she said as she cleaned up the mess he had made of dinner. "He never told me he hated green beans," she mumbled through her tears.

Hastily, she cleaned the mess he had made on the bedroom floor and put on her work uniform.

Three

The Office Bar & Grill was crowded as usual when Danielle arrived. JC was already hustling around taking care of customers and preparing for the after work crowd. Her usual electric personality charged the room with energy and life. She waved a hello to Danielle.

Danielle waved back and headed toward the small office where they put their jackets and purses. JC entered the room behind her.

"Not again Danielle," she said, reaching for her arm.

"Ouch," Danielle flinched when JC touched her shoulder. "It's nothing, really. I'm fine".

"Yeah, right! That jerk. Why don't you leave him before he does something worse," JC said, shaking her head.

Some one called from the dining room "Hey, JC, you working, or what?"

"Be right there. Keep your shirt on," she called back. "We'll talk later Danielle. Are you sure you're okay? We can call Amanda in if you need the night off."

"No. JC, I'm fine, besides I need the money," she said putting on her red vest apron that was part of their uniform. "I'll be right out."

JC put a coaster in front of Danielle and poured two glasses of brandy over the rocks. "What are you going to do Danielle? Why don't you move in with me? I have a spare room. I'd enjoy the company. What do you say? Please?" She reached out and held Danielle's hand.

"I can't, JC. He'd just come after me. Remember after he broke—" she quickly corrected the phrase "—ah, when I broke my arm? He harassed me here, everywhere. He won't leave me alone. He'll be banging down your door every night and disrupting things here, like last time."

"We'll get a restraining order on him. He wouldn't dare bother you then. Come on Danielle, I worry about you. You can't go on like this."

"I appreciate your concern JC. I'll think about it. I promise," she said.

They finished their drinks and JC gave her a ride home. A light glowed in the upstairs apartment window. "He's watching TV," she said as JC stopped the car. "He's up."

"Call me if he starts anything." JC pleaded. "I'll call the police and come right over. Promise?" she asked, holding Danielle's arm. "Matter of fact why don't I come up with you just to see how he reacts?"

"Oh, no, JC, that would for sure set him off. You know how he likes his privacy."

"Yeah, so he can beat the crap out of you without any witnesses," she said.

Danielle sighed, she knew her friend was right, "Randy has had time to sleep it off so he would probably be all right," she told JC.

"Then do this. When you get in dial my number and hang up, then if you need me you only need to punch redial, if he jumps all over you, you only need to hit one button instead of trying to dial my whole number. Will you at least do that?"

Danielle looked at the concern in her friend's eyes. *She really is a friend like I've never had.* "I will JC, please don't worry. Everything will be fine. I'll talk to you tomorrow, okay?"

"Okay, but call if you need me." She said again.

What if she wasn't okay? What if he was in a worse rage than before? She walked slowly to the entryway and tiptoed around the homeless woman who had just lately started sleeping in the shelter of the stairwell. The woman stirred briefly and Danielle climbed the stairs listening to the creaking groan of every step. The exertion made her right rib cage throb where she had hit the doorframe when Randy bounced her off it earlier that day. She could hear canned laughter and the nasal twang of Peg Bundy. Randy was watching a *"Married With Children"* rerun, one of his favorite sit-coms. She felt his mood must have improved or he would be blasting rock music. Cautiously, she opened the door. The TV was on but Randy was snoring peacefully with his head twisted in an awkward angle as he slept. Danielle tiptoed past him and into their bedroom, undressing and slipping into bed without disturbing him. She breathed a sigh of relief as she slid under the covers and closed her eyes.

~ * ~

Home alone again in the small apartment after Randy left to run what he called "errands", Danielle studied her image in the mirror. She had bruises on her arms and hip, the large burn on her left forearm, and the swollen lip and bruised cheek. "I look like a refugee from a boxing match," she said aloud. No, she vowed Randy had his last chance. She would find a way to get safely away from him. JC had promised to help her. She could hear her friends scolding, begging, "Please get out before he kills you, Danielle. My apartment building is secured with a gate and the doorman watches out for all of us that live there. Randy won't even know you are there."

"What about work, he'll come there? He'll follow me." Danielle protested between sobs.

"No, you won't work except when I do. I'll clear it with Brady, he'll understand. We have Trish or Amanda one of them can take over a couple of your shifts if need be I'm sure. Okay? Please say you will. We'll go to the Marshal and get a restraining order on him," JC had said.

Danielle dragged the big blue suitcase from under the bed. She tossed it on the bed and opened it. I never thought I would be doing this again, at least not for the reasons I am. Why are men such idiots? Why can't they have a social drink and stay in control of their minds and actions? I don't know one man, haven't known *any* man yet who chooses life over alcohol. Is it the whole world or just the people in my life?

Danielle opened the dresser drawer, pulled most of her things out, and shoved them in the suitcase. *I better leave some so that Randy won't become suspicious if he decided to look.* Standing on the rickety old chair in front of the closet to see the top shelf to be sure nothing of hers was left up there she needed to be sure Randy hadn't put anything there. On the far right hand side, she felt something. Tugging it to the front of the shelf she discovered it was a backpack. *Where did this come from? I never saw this before.* She laid it on the bed and opened it. Packed inside it were textbooks from the Colorado School of Metallurgical Mining and Engineering and some vials neatly labeled Hydrogen Cyanide. *Randolph Ord III* was written in the cover and it was dated two years earlier.

Glancing at the highlighted passages as she flipped through the book, seeing the whole book had passages that had been highlighted, she realized Randy had to have completed his studies. A folded sheet of paper tucked in the back confirmed her thoughts. It was a degree in Metallurgical Engineering from the school. Why hadn't he mentioned this? Why didn't he have a job if he had the credentials to get one? Danielle carefully refolded the paper and placed it back in the book. Holding one of the vials up to the light, she saw it contained some liquid. There is still Hydrogen Cyanide in this vial. Somewhere in the far reaches of her mind she vaguely remembered the chemical being used for something she was sure was quite sinister. It made her shudder. *The Holocaust.* That was it. This was what they used in the gas chambers on the Jews. It was lethal. It was used as a gas to kill.

Her mind was swirling with facts and information, the murder mystery she had read—it was used in a candle. It was…it was…exactly what she needed. Carefully she put the other vials back in the backpack; chances are he wouldn't notice that one was missing. Perhaps she could use it before he had a chance to discover it was gone. In her craft room she hid the vial under a pile of wax blocks. Hurriedly, she finished packing the suitcase to take it to the small storage cubicle in the basement. They never used it because the place was so damp and dirty. Randy would never look there.

The basement door creaked and groaned as she opened it. The musty dead air stung her nostrils. She flipped the light switch on the wall in the stairwell. Something scurried from the glow of the single bare bulb hanging above the foot of the wooden stairway.

"Ugh, mice," she groaned as she brushed past cobwebs. Hurriedly she wiped at the rusted plates on the storage bins looking for her apartment number. Finding the right one, she jammed the key into the lock and twisted. The key did not budge the rusted lock.

"Damn." She looked around for something to spray on the lock. On a dusty shelf by the stairs she saw the blue and yellow can of WD40, "Yes." She breathed heavily, grabbed the can and shook it. "Good, there's still some in it." She pressed the nozzle and the the spray hissed toward the lock. Then she sprayed the key, and put the can back amongst the cobwebs on the shelf and tried the lock again. The key turned easily now. She lifted the heavy lid and slid the suitcase inside.

"Who's down there?" a voice bellowed from the stairwell.

Danielle jumped as though the storage bin had bitten her. She swallowed and her heart returned back down into her chest cavity and then she turned, fear ripping at her like a wild beast. Silver hair glowed like a halo above stoop-shouldered Mr. Groton. He was the caretaker Mrs. People had hired earlier this year when vandals started painting graffiti in the hallways and breaking windows.

She inhaled a breath of damp moldy air, "Just me, Danielle," she called to the shadow. "Putting some things in storage that's all," she tried to make her voice sound nonchalant.

"Just checking missy sorry if'n I startled ya, thought ya might be one o'them dang hooligans," he rasped.

"It's okay Mr. Groton, I'm coming up now anyway."

"Be sure to turn out the lights," he said as he shuffled off down the hallway. She heard his door creak open and click shut. A dead bolt slid home then silence except for a TV somewhere. Something skittered across her foot and she remembered the mice. She bolted for the stairway and took the steps two at a time. Quickly she flicked the light switch and shut the door.

Down the hall and up the stairs to her apartment she dashed. Before Randy came home, she would make good use of that vial. He had gotten used to the candles she lit all over to rid the tiny apartment of the stale smell of beer, cigarettes and marijuana smell constantly in the air. Now she would make a special one just for him. She would light it some night when he was passed out drunk from one of his all night parties. She would have to do some research first. She did not want to be discovered as one of the bodies in the apartment. If she melted the wax and formed the candle, she could sprinkle the cyanide on it while it hardened and then when she lit it the air would become lethal. How long would it take? Would she have time to leave the apartment and escape its effect? How long before the odor produced would dissipate and leave no traces? She had some very real questions before she dared put her plan into action.

~ * ~

Danielle opened the letter from the Industrial Scientific Corporation anticipating the information she needed to know. The Data Sheet contained a few things she worried about, especially the hazard warning "Highly Flammable". How could she incorporate it into her candle if it was flammable? How did they do it in that mystery book she had read? What was the name of that book? She read on. *Used in the leaching of precious metals, i.e. gold, chemical plants, insecticides.* That would explain why Randy had obtained some from the college. *But, if it is so dangerous, how could he have gotten vials of it to keep for his personal use?* She had read somewhere that college students experimented with it as a drug to replace heroin or something, but Randy didn't do hard drugs. He had assured her of that many times. He was, however, a rebel, that was very much a fact. A fact that she liked in him since she herself was the opposite, never daring to take risks, usually fading into the background like some nondescript plant or wallpaper.

She examined the vial of cyanide, and checked it against the data sheet. *Hydrogen cyanide is a colorless to a pale blue liquid or gas. It has a distinct odor resembling bitter almonds that only some people can detect.* Did she dare risk smelling it?

She cracked the vial open and then closed it. She detected no odor. *Hydrogen cyanide is particularly dangerous because of its toxic/asphyxiating effects on all life requiring oxygen to survive. HCN combines with the enzymes in tissue associated with cellular oxidation. What this means is it interferes with the oxygen available to the tissues causing death by asphyxia. If the poisoning occurs rapidly, e.g., as a result of extremely high concentrations in the air, there is no time for symptoms to develop and exposed persons may then suddenly collapse and die. This suspension only lasts while the cyanide is present. Upon its removal, normal function is restored provided death has not occurred."* She shuddered reading the final line. She would have to be extremely careful Cyanide could also be taken up through the skin.

What am I thinking? Do I hate him enough to risk my life to get rid of him? The fumes will dissipate and no one will ever know, unless they do an autopsy. The data sheet also gave the toxicity levels and resulting conditions that were symptoms. She would put enough into that candle to be sure it was highly toxic. She would destroy all this information once the plan was in motion. It would be nice to know more about the method she could use to integrate it into the candle. She didn't want to be around long enough to breathe any of the fumes. If she put it in the candle wax while she was melting it, it would surely produce a lethal dose.

Danielle knew how long the wax would stay pliable and she had been experimenting with a technique to mold candles into animal shapes while it was still warm. It gave the animals a primitive, almost native quality. Perhaps she could use gloves and work the cyanide into a small portion that would be the top of the candle. She would get one of those paper respiratory masks to protect her and work with the window open. She was sure she had figured out the *how*. Now to figure out the *when*. It had to be soon. She could no longer tolerate Randy and his abuse.

She folded the letter and put it back in the envelope. Her stomach lurched as she pondered her plans. She started to sob, "Oh, Mom, if only you were here. I see no way to get out of this situation without doing something totally drastic and stupid. I don't want to start over again. I don't want to run again. He said he'd find me no matter where I went. I have no one to turn to." Danielle folded her arms around her stomach. It felt like her insides were being ripped apart by some roaring dragon. The tears rolled down her cheeks and splashed on her jeans. She rocked and cried. Hugging herself she prayed an answer would come from somewhere to rescue her. "I'd rather die than live like this," she sobbed into the dead still air of the apartment.

Exhausted, she forced herself to stand up and hide the letter behind some of her books on the wooden shelf over her worktable. "No use crying—this is the only way," she said stiffening her spine and wiping furiously at the remaining tears.

Four

"Come on Ruth you've got to help me out. I've got a chance to make something of myself, but I need to get dried out and I don't think I can do it alone. Please! I'll never ask again. I promise." Randy was desperate; his sister was the last resort.

Ruth glared at Randy. "Give me one good reason why I should help you? You're nothing but a pain in the ass to everyone who knows you. Hell, you can't even keep a girlfriend. They all know you aren't worth shit. I am done giving you hand outs while Mom and Dad pray for the prodigal son's return. Their baby boy can do no wrong. I've had it with you. Out! Now!"

"One lousy chance Ruth, that's all I'm asking." Randy begged.

"What did you do with the money I gave you to dry out last time? You didn't even make it home before you blew everything. Yes, I know all about that. I know how hard you fell off the wagon that time. No, you will not get another dime from this family. You'll have to find another way. Now, goodbye. I have a company to run since you've seen fit to turn your back on it." Ruth opened her office door. "Don't make me call security."

Randy flung his jacket over his shoulder. "Thanks, Sis, I'll remember this. I should have known better than to ask you for anything," he said as he stormed out of her office.

He was certain Ruth watched him get on his Harley. Squealing his tires out of the parking lot and back onto the highway, he vowed he would turn his life around without her help, and show her he could. Danielle was all he needed. At this point, he sure didn't need Ruth's high and mighty attitude trying to lay a guilt trip on him. She wasn't to blame if he didn't get his life on track. But he knew that she wished he would drive his Harley into the nearest gorge. The long drive back to Durango from Colorado Springs only served to increase his anger. The door to the apartment rattled the casement as he slammed it shut. Danielle jumped at the sudden noise.

"Hi, where have you been? I've been worried," she said.

"Why? I'm a big boy. I can take care of myself. You just take care of you and stay to hell out of my business for once." He opened the refrigerator and took out a beer, popped the lid and guzzled half the can before he stopped. Then wiping his sleeve across his mouth, he fell into the easy chair and clicked on the TV. "Aren't you going to work today?"

"Yes, but not until six. You know that."

"Oh, so now I'm supposed to be a fucking mind reader too?"

"What is the matter? What did I do this time? Can't you say one decent word to me? Ever?" she asked, tears welling up in her eyes.

"Sorry, had a bad day," he mumbled.

"Well, don't take it out on me."

Randy tossed the beer can across the room. Stood up and glared at her. She cowered. "I'm outta here," he said as he crossed the room. The force of the door, as it slammed, shook the whole apartment.

Randy jumped down hard on the kick-start and the bike responded with a loud roar. He tore out of the parking lot. His only choice for money now was to make one more run for Shorty unless he would just loan him the money, which Randy doubted. At least he wouldn't have to depend on family then.

He immediately hated the way he had just treated Danielle. *I love that girl with all my heart and I treat her like shit every time we're together. What the hell is the matter with me anyway? Shorty should be at The Italian Inn by now. I'll get the money from him and check in to that treatment center tonight. I'll have them notify Danielle. Dear sister Ruth won't hold me hostage.*

Five

Danielle opened the door to a tall older woman nervously clutching a handbag and fiddling with a key chain. "Can I help you?" she said thinking that obviously this socialite was lost. She sure did not fit in with the lower side of Durango.

"I'm looking for Randy Ord," the woman said looking past Danielle into the apartment. "Do I have the right place?"

"Yes, this is Randy's apartment. He isn't here right now."

"Do you know when to expect him back?" she asked sharply.

"Who wants to know?"

"I'm his sister, Ruth Ord. He gave me this address when he visited me a week ago. Can you tell me where I can find him, or when he'll return?"

"I don't know where he is or when he'll be home. He took off two days ago. He does that some times. Comes back when he feels like it."

"Then you don't know if he'll be back at all?" Ruth asked abruptly.

"Would you like to come in?" Danielle didn't know Randy had any family. He had never told her of any and when she asked, he said his parents died in a car accident and he did not have any other family. She would like to see what Ruth Ord was about.

"I guess I could. I could use a drink of water. I haven't stopped anywhere since I left Colorado Springs."

Danielle took a glass out of the cupboard and let the water run to make sure it was cold and fresh. Durango's water was some of the purest and best tasting she had ever had. Ms. Ord scrutinized the apartment and brushed off a chair before perching on the edge of it like a bird ready to take flight.

"Excuse the mess," Danielle apologized. "I work nights and actually just got up a little bit ago."

"Oh, no problem. So, you are Randy's girlfriend or live in or what?"

"Randy and I have been living together just over a year. Was he expecting you?"

"I hardly think so. He came to see me to ask for money. Something about going to get dried out."

If that was where Randy had gone why didn't he tell her? She was confused. "Would you like a cup of coffee, or anything?"

"Yes, I could use a cup. So, you don't know where Randy is?"

"He doesn't always tell me where he's going." Danielle said, pouring Ms Ord a cup of coffee. "Did you give Randy the money he asked for?"

"No, I sure didn't. I am tired of giving him money. Last time he said he was going to dry out, too. I guess the road back was too rocky because he never made it to the next town before he drank most of it away. He called me from the drunk tank in some little burg. No, I wasn't about to throw good money after bad."

"Then why are you here, if you decided he isn't worth the effort?"

"It's not that we don't have the money. He would inherit a fortune if our parents were gone." Ruth Ord eyed her with a shadow of mistrust in her eyes

"I thought there was a way I could help him without actually giving him the money directly. That isn't exactly the truth either. He doesn't deserve one red cent. He never worked for any of it. Mother handed him every thing he ever wanted. Her precious baby boy could do not wrong. But our father is terribly ill. Father adores the ground Randy tramples on. I wanted to see if he'd come home to see him. It would mean so much to daddy. It may even help him in his recovery. I would pay for his treatment at a…" Ruth Ord suddenly seemed at a loss for words.

Danielle watched as Ruth Ord fidgeted and cleared her throat. She took a drink of coffee but her eyes had a far away look like they were lost somewhere in her thoughts

"I suppose he would call it a bribe, but I would do anything for my father whether he appreciates it or not," Ruth said.

Danielle was shocked at this revelation. She wasn't quite sure how to respond to Ruth Ord's statement. "I'm so sorry to hear that your father is ill. I will certainly tell Randy when he comes home."

"Don't bother. He won't care. He hates our mother so much he would do anything to cause her more pain."

Danielle listened quietly while Ruth Ord described the rift between Randy and his parents. The times she tried to help him, the jobs he ran away from because his mother kept using his attempts at job hunting to track him down and try to get him back home. Danielle didn't offer much input into Ruth Ord's vision of her and Randy's life. Ruth seemed too preoccupied with all that she had done for Randy over the years. Danielle didn't think it mattered one way or another to Ruth what his life was like now. She heard the "I, I, I" in her monologue of deeds done and kudos earned. Ruth was so wrapped up in self-pity. Danielle knew Randy was not the issue here. It was Ruth's position in the family, her parents that mattered. Randy was a pawn to be used... however he could further her position with the company and her parents.

By the time Ruth Ord left, Danielle was more confused then ever. She had a completely new picture of Randy Ord. He was heir to millions. His family was filthy rich. He'd lied about them. He didn't want her to know or was it he didn't want them to find out about her. Was she not good enough for their blue blood? Why the pretense at being a pauper? She wasn't sure just what she would do with this information. Ruth Ord begged her not to tell Randy she was there. She said she would contact him by mail, figuring he would not want to see her anyway after she had refused his latest request for money.

Maybe I could use this to my advantage. He has abused me enough that it's time I turn the tables on him for a change. If he would marry me, at least then I'd have a chance of getting some of that money. I deserve it for putting up with him. If I was pregnant he might. *No, Randy, I won't kill you, I'll only make you wish I had.*

Determination squared her shoulders and caused her a flash of excitement. Danielle began tidying up the apartment and took a long hard look at her overall appearance. Randy would see a new Danielle. A devoted, loving companion that doted on his every need even if that meant entertaining his party friends. She knew she had her work cut out for her, but she would get Randy to marry her. Who knows? Maybe an off spring would settle him down and make him want the child to have a chance to get to know the grandparents.

Six

"Hey Randy, long time no see," Shorty Delegano said as he stood and came around the desk toward him. "Come in. Come in. What can I do for you? Here sit, can I get you something? Coffee? A drink—anything?" He waved his arm toward the back bar lining one end of the spacious office.

"Actually, nothing. I came to ask you a favor," Randy said hedging against what he was trying to say.

"Hey, Randy. You know you can count on me. What is it you need? A quick job to make some extra cash?" Delegano asked, returning to his chair behind the big oak desk and picking up a cigar, he had been chewing on.

"I, ah, well sir…"

"Knock off the sir shit, Randy. You can call me Shorty. We know each other a long time. Shorty works for me. What do ya say?"

"Okay. Sure. Ah, Shorty," Randy paused for a long moment not knowing where to start. He had rehearsed the speech repeatedly in his mind on the way up to the plush resort community of Lake Viacetto Village, but somehow the words could not get from his mind to his tongue.

"Spit it out boy, what's the scoop?"

Randy blurted out. "I need a loan Shorty. Not a big one, just enough to get into a treatment program to dry out, that's all." Immediately he hung his head afraid to look at Delegano.

Shorty Delegano broke into coarse laughter that raked across Randy's insides like finger nails on a black board. Chipmunk cheeks squeezed Shorty's eyes forcing tears to run down his face while he laughed. Randy waited. Finally Delegano dried his eyes with a white handkerchief.

"Look Mr. Delegano I've got a chance at a legit job. I can't do this any more. I want out now," Randy said. Sweat dampened his back and underarms. He knew this was a risky idea, but he had to get out while he still had a chance at a decent life. He loved Danielle and he did not want to lose her.

"Sure kid, sure. But you know how they feel upstairs about anyone quitting," Shorty said. Randy did know it all too well. He had seen enough to know that anything he said to the wrong people could bring a lot of trouble down on Shorty's organization. He did not care. He needed to take the chance to get clear before he got into trouble with the law and lost Danielle forever.

"Listen, maybe I could talk to them for you if you could you do me one last favor first. You're all trained; you know the route and the drop-off points—if you can do one more run for us, we'll clear it with the big boys. What do you say, kid? One more run, that's all. Then we're history. Look at it this way, you'll get the money you need and won't have to pay back a stupid loan at the interest rates we charge and you're home free. Okay?" The stocky little man held out a pudgy hand to Randy.

Randy took the hand and agreed to one more run. "This is it though; this is the very last run. Got that?" He hoped his voice sounded a lot more firm than he felt at the moment.

Shorty agreed.

That was almost too easy. Why had Randy been so afraid? Shorty seemed very happy to help him get out. That unnerved Randy; he needed to do something, some kind of insurance policy against Shorty's thugs doing anything stupid. He needed to get some evidence against them into the right hands so he would have a safeguard in the event they tried something. He knew where the Oxycontin tablets were coming from. He knew the drop-off points, the warehouses that accepted them and he knew names. Certainly he could put together something that guaranteed they wouldn't touch him or Danielle for fear of what he would do with the information he knew. At the same time, he worried that they may not let him leave because of the information he was privy to. What if they tried to kill him before he could tell anyone? He needed a plan and he needed to act quickly.

First, he needed to talk to his sister, Ruth. There was one more area of his life that needed cleaning up if he hoped to salvage his relationship with Danielle and gain the strength he needed to get on with his life. He had a job interview lined up. He wasn't about to screw that up. It was a good job. It would put him back in the mainstream of life where he belonged. Yes, Ruth had to see that he was trying to do something decent with his life.

Seven

When Danielle got home from work, Randy was sitting in front of the TV as usual. He looked up and smiled like he had only seen her that morning, and was waiting for her return. Three weeks had passed since she last saw him.

"Hi babe. How was work?" he asked.

"The same as every other day, in the long stretch since I've seen you last." She was angry yet glad he hadn't been around. While she hadn't had to cater to his every need or fear a temper tantrum, she could relax. Did she even dare ask where he had been? Would he go ballistic and slap her around or what? She was never sure with him anymore.

"I suppose you wonder where I've been," he said.

"Why should I, you never told me before, why tell me now?"

"Look honey, I'm sorry. I have been so screwed up I just haven't been myself. Can you forgive me? I will make it better for you, I promise."

He sounded sincere and at this point she did not care; she wanted him to marry her and she was willing to play along with him to get what she wanted for a change. "Like all the other times you promised the same thing Randy?"

"I swear sweetheart this time it will be different. Come on give a guy a chance will you?"

"Okay, Randy. Okay, you want a chance. Here's what I want. I want you to marry me; I want you to get a real job. I want you to become what we dreamed of together two years ago. That's what I want." Danielle didn't know where her courage came from; she had never talked to him that way before. She had never asked him for anything.

All of sudden she thought, what do I have to lose? If he turned belligerent she would just walk out and never come back. He would never know she was pregnant. He would never see his child or know he was a father. That would be the end of it. She had only found out she was pregnant last week. Even JC didn't know yet.

Since ovarian cancer had killed her mother, Danielle had made yearly visits to the doctor. Her mom too had been told she was pregnant. When the doctors discovered she wasn't, it was too late and she was dead in three months. Danielle had been relieved to learn she was only pregnant.

She had thought about using the child as leverage to get Randy to marry her. In the end, she decided she didn't want him if she had to force him. No matter how much he was worth she couldn't do that.

"Okay Danielle, you set the date. We'll get married tomorrow if you want. I promise to make things right. What do you say, honey? I love you, you have to know that."

Danielle *didn't* know that. She thought she did once but not after the events of the last few months. She wasn't sure of anything between them anymore. "We'll see Randy, let's just see how things go for the next week. Then I'll decide."

"Great. I promise you, you won't regret it. Now, come over here and give me a big welcome home kiss and let's talk." He reached out to her and she found she could not resist. His charm had always had power over her.

"There is something else you should know Randy," she said pushing back from his embrace. He looked at her quizzically.

"So spill it, did you find some one else, what? You know you can tell me anything." At least he sounded sincere for this moment.

"I'm pregnant," she blurted out.

"That's great," he said. "At least I think so, don't you?" He grabbed her and hugged her close to him. "That's the best news I believe I ever heard. How long have you known?"

"Actually, I just got confirmation from the doctor yesterday, I'm four months, at least, he figures."

"We'll have to get a bigger place," he said.

Standing up and looking around the tiny apartment, he measured, with his arms, crib areas and she was not sure what else. Danielle could not believe what she was hearing. He was actually happy about the news. She waited for the bombshell she was sure would follow. It never came. They talked half the night about names, would it be boy or girl and who cared, as long as the baby was healthy. They fell asleep in each other's arms.

Things were still happy and light in the morning. Randy was happy and content.

"Can I ask where you have been," she said as she set his eggs and bacon in front of him.

"Would you believe I went to make enough money to go and get dried out? Well, I did. Danielle, I am so sick of what I have been doing to our relationship and myself. I can't live with that anymore. So, as soon as I got paid I checked in to the center in Boulder. I have a good job waiting for me when I get back."

"Randy, that's great." She said and she meant every word of it. "Why didn't you let me know? Why didn't you call or something?"

"I just wasn't sure I could actually go through with it and I didn't want you to be disappointed"

Danielle could not wait to tell JC the good news.

Eight

The smell of fresh cinnamon rolls emanated from the Bakery downstairs. Danielle loved waking to the scent of freshly baked bread and rolls every morning. It seemed that some days it was the only reason to wake up at all. It brought back childhood memories of Saturdays when her mother would bake. Always on Saturday the noon meal would be pudding and fresh rolls hot out of the oven. Her father was never home for lunch on Saturdays so they had a special treat instead of a real meal. At least her father would not call pudding and fresh bread a real meal. The bakery downstairs reminded her of many things and she loved it even if the heat was unbearable in the summer because of it.

Danielle stretched; it didn't get much better than this. She never actually got fresh rolls for breakfast; the smell was intoxicating enough. She knew the empty calories and the sweetness were not what she craved, but the smell gave her impetus enough to begin her day.

When she had first moved in with Randy, there had been a robbery in the bakery downstairs. They were awakened in the middle of the night with the police banging on the door of their apartment. Danielle had never been so scared in all her life. It seemed the thief had used the skylight outside their apartment to get into the bakery. Their open bedroom windows faced out onto the roof. The police thought that perhaps the thief had come through their apartment to escape. Clutching the blankets to her Danielle had watched the flashlights outside searching the rooftop for clues. There were no screens on the widows and the breeze moved the thin lace panel curtains. The voices drifted in, blurring as she listened to the officer asking Randy if he heard or saw anything suspicious. What time did they go to bed? Is the door always locked? If someone ran out through it would it relock or did it take a key. Danielle's mind swirled with the thought of her privacy being invaded by some stranger, some man intent on breaking the law. What if they had awakened and saw him? Would he have killed them? Randy put his arm around her and she buried her face in his shoulder. She felt like she had been raped. She started to cry and shake. Randy led her and the officer to the living room. He wrapped the blanket around her tightly and sat her on the couch. The officer finished his questions, wrote a telephone number on a card, and gave it to Randy as he let him out the door into the hallway. Apparently, the police had roused everyone in the building because Danielle saw people milling in the hallway outside her door. She rarely thought about the incident anymore since the owner of the bakery put a solid roof in where the skylight had been and the fire escape the thief had used was now padlocked and only accessible from the roof top, not below.

Today though was great. She couldn't wait to go tell JC that she and Randy were to be married. She hoped her best friend would agree to be her maid of honor. "Mrs. Randy Ord." She played with the sound of the title. "Yes that sounds great!"

Danielle made coffee and poured a tall glass of juice for herself. She took it out on the back steps to watch the sun come up over the mountains. She loved the Colorado landscape. Not at all like the bluffs, she was used to in Wisconsin. The shapes the sun and shadows played over the mountains, the way the clouds seem to scrape their bellies on the mountaintops, the early morning mist playing tag with the sun as it chased across the valley and floated in and out of the peaks mesmerized her. The show was never the same. Minute by minute the landscape changed. She strained hard to try to see the elk herd she knew was winding its way down the mountain at this time of the morning. The traffic was starting to pick up on the street below.

"Maybe I should go get some fresh pastries to celebrate this morning," she said to the magpie helping himself to the crumbs strewn around the base of the dumpster.

Nine

"JC, I can hardly believe it myself. Will you be my maid of honor? We are going to get married right away," Danielle said.

"Danielle, are you sure this is what you want? What if he falls off the wagon? What if the old Randy returns, before the ink is dry on the marriage license? Then what? Think about what you're doing, please," JC said.

"Don't worry, JC, I know what I'm doing. My child will have a father. He will be taken care of whether or not Randy and I remain married." Danielle gave JC a hug. "It'll be all right you'll see. Now will you stand up for me or will I have to take the court clerk to be my maid of honor?"

"You know I'll stand up for you. You're my friend. I just don't want you to make a mistake you may not live to regret, that's all."

"You're such a worry wart. Lighten up. I told you Randy has changed. He's different. Besides I will keep my candle handy should things turn sour."

"Danielle you couldn't. You wouldn't use that blasted thing. I thought it was a joke, I couldn't believe you actually made the dumb thing. You should get rid of it now before someone accidentally lights it."

"Oh JC, who would do that? I'm the one who is obsessed with candles. No one else even seems to notice they're in the room. No, I've hidden it away. No one will accidentally light it. If it's lit it will be me, and I'll have a damn good reason for doing it."

"Okay, you let me know the date and time and I'll be your maid of honor with bells on girl."

"Great! Thanks JC, I knew I could count on you," Danielle said.

JC shook her head and started clearing tables for the next rush that always came into the bar & grill; the after work crowd of suits and secretaries unwinding after a day of moving and dealing. Danielle liked the crowd and the talk was always lively and made the early evening go quickly. She couldn't wait to get home to Randy. The new Randy. They were a team again.

It seemed as though all her plans were back on track and she silently crossed her fingers hoping that JC was just paranoid about her future with Randy. She's such a worrywart, Danielle thought. Always looking at the clouds, never searching for the silver lining.

Well, that wasn't exactly true. JC knew what she wanted and she was working hard to get it. She was cautious, but not paranoid, not usually. Danielle had the slightest twinge of uncertainty in her own mind, but she wouldn't let her doubts destroy this moment of happiness no matter how short-lived it might be.

She busied herself with setting up the salad bar and tables. As her mother used to say, "Don't borrow trouble." Danielle was determined that it was time for the universe to give up the happiness she had waited so long to find. It was her turn. She deserved it. She vigorously rubbed at the spots on the table like she was trying to erase the spots from her life as well. "I will have it. I will have happiness," she resolved under her breath.

"What did you say?" JC Asked as she headed to the kitchen with a bucket of dirty dishes.

"Oh nothing, nothing at all. Just clearing my throat," Danielle lied.

Ten

Sitting in the corridor of the courthouse waiting for the judge unnerved Randy. Getting married was a step he had not planned on at this point in his life. He did not want to lose Danielle, yet he was not sure he was ready for marriage. How had she managed to talk him into this, and why now?

Maybe she thought it would change him. Change him for what? He had no intentions of becoming a yuppie like some others he knew. JC and Danielle seemed to think this was a party the way they were giggling and carrying on like two schoolgirls.

Who was this JC anyway? Danielle only worked with her. Danielle probably didn't know anyone else who could stand up for her; that must be it. Ah well, what did he care? Skeet had agreed to be his best man. Best man? *Shit*. Normally he would not have let him clean his shoes, but what did it matter who stood up for him? It was just a formality, someone to sign the stupid papers, a witness to what he had done. He and Danielle had lived together for years. Why suddenly wasn't that good enough? Who gets married now days anyway? It's what she wanted.

I guess I owe her something for putting up with me. His palms were starting to sweat and he could feel the tiny beads forming around his hairline. Why was he so nervous? It wasn't the end of the world. If you believe the romance movies, it is a brand new, exciting beginning. *Yeah right!*

The door to the judge's chamber opened and the bailiff called out, "Danielle Maynard and Randolph Ord III, this way please. The judge is ready for you now," he said solemnly.

Danielle smiled and winked at Randy. She slipped her small hand into his and walked with him to the open door.

Eleven

Randy sat in the small restaurant. He watched people kicking up little dust clouds as they walked up and down the powder-dry street. The vibrant colors of the Mexican serapes stood out against the dullness of the parched earth and the vibrant blue sky. The town had a gaiety about it that belied the depression of the people as they struggled with the land to eke out a living.

He thought how the town replicated his own life and troubles. His life had such bleakness a few days before. Now, a ray of sunshine, hope, with the baby on the way and a job in his future, things had brightness of the Mexican costume and his past the barrenness of the parched land. The New Mexico landscape and people of this small town made him think they had not left Mexico at all. Only the mapmakers had decided that this was a *New* Mexico.

Randy pushed his empty plate to the center of the table and took a pad of paper out of his backpack. He uncapped his pen and sat, forming words in his mind. How would he explain to his mother that he was redesigning his life to include the woman he loved and the child she would bear in the near future? How would he make her see that he had a job offer in a field he had trained for in college? Could he make her understand he liked his life now and wanted to include them in it, but not on their terms?

His mother was so demanding. She would decide he did not know how to design his own life. She would harass him to return home and follow her directives. He wanted desperately to have his father as his friend as he had always been. Not to the exclusion of his mother, but if she would be part of his life on his terms, then, then he could come home. They could be part of his family. How could he get his mother to realize that he would only return home on his own terms?

He couldn't, no, he wouldn't live under her thumb anymore. How could he make her understand that? He started the letter only to crumble the paper, toss it into his empty plate, and start again.

Why was it so hard for him to say what was on his mind, to be decisive when it came to his mother? He began the letter again carefully choosing his words. He told them he was married and that soon they would be grandparents. He told them he loved them both and wanted them to be part of his family. He had a job they would be proud of, but that he was determined to live his life the way he planned it. If they could accept that, he would be able to come home and bring his family with him.

"I love you Mom & Dad, hope to see you soon." He signed the letter. Addressed the envelope and slid it into his pocket. He finished his coffee, paid for his meal, got on the Harley, and headed south.

In the small New Mexican town of Los Montoyes he stopped at the tiny post office and slipped the letter in the mail slot then climbed on his Harley and headed back toward Durango, Colorado, hoping his parents would for once, understand his need to be his own person. He hoped they would give him and Danielle space to do that.

He did not trust that his mother would. He felt the trip to New Mexico was worth the time and energy to insure she would not find him just yet. He knew she would try. She always did. Beatrice Ord was a determined woman. When she wanted something, she would let nothing stand in the way of her getting it. *I am as stubborn as she is he thought with a wry smile.*

The breeze against his face felt good. As he headed home he hoped that was a good omen, which would cause things to blow in his favor for a change.

Twelve

Beatrice Ord clutched the letter to her chest; she recognized the handwriting immediately. The unmistakable, round, perfectly formed letters, though shaky were definitely Randy's. She held the letter to her heart and uttered a "Thank you Lord, no matter what it says."

She sat down in her favorite easy chair by the fireplace, her hands trembling with anticipation. She turned the letter over and over in her hands, afraid to open it. It had been a year since Randy had last initiated a contact with them. She scrutinized the cancellation stamp, Los Montoyes, New Mexico. She went to the bookcase, pulled down the huge atlas and opened it to New Mexico. It took a few minutes to find the tiny town. She looked for major highways that led to or near it. Where was he really, she wondered. She knew in her heart it wasn't mailed from the place he actually lived. She closed the atlas and replaced it on the book shelf

Slowly she lifted the letter opener and slid it into the space at the corner of the envelope. Cautiously and deliberately, she cut it open, hesitatingly removing the single folded sheet from it cloistered space.

She sunk into the desk chair and unfolded the letter, her hands trembling with dread and anticipation.

"Dear Mom & Dad, I hope you are well. Please read this whole letter before you react."

It started out slowly and she could tell deliberate. She could feel that he must have weighed each word before he put it on the paper. Her heart fluttered between elation and despair. She loved her only son more than life itself. How could he shut her out of his life so completely? She needed him so. She needed him to validate her reason for being. She gave him everything. She had struggled with his father at every turn trying to direct his path through the tangles of growing up. How could he desert her? She held her breath and continued reading the letter.

Married? Grandchild? She read on. *"Don't look for me please mother, I'll come home eventually, I need space now."*

Anger replaced her earlier joy and fear. *How could he marry a woman I've never met?* How could he? *Without my approval. Without my blessing? What kind of woman was she?* She had to be after his money. He is so stupid in affairs of the heart. He never could judge people. In that respect, he is like his father. He probably married her for spite. We will see how much it will take for her to leave him. Those kinds of people can be bought. You just need to know how to deal with them. The grandchild is Randy's and we will pay her for him too. I will have Randy and his son; it will be a son. The Ords always have a son first. It's in the genes. Yes, a strong healthy boy. I have always wanted another son. *Yes, some good will come out of this mistake, I will see to that.*

She folded the letter and replaced it in the envelope then hid it in a small box at the back of her desk drawer. No point in worrying Randolph about this matter, she told herself. What he does not know cannot hurt him.

She closed the drawer and dialed the private investigator's number.

"Beatrice Ord here," she snapped at the secretary "I need to talk to Mr. Cutcheon immediately."

"Beatrice Ord here Mr. Cutcheon. I have another job for you. Stop by first thing in the morning and I will fill you in. Yes, all right, see you at 10:00 a.m."

She replaced the telephone in its cradle, straightened her desk, and rang for the housekeeper.

"Bring me one of my tranquilizers and some tea please. I have a dreadful headache," she said.

The housekeeper did as she was told. Mrs. Ord printed Los Montoyes, New Mexico on a tablet along with the date the letter was mailed.

She thought about Randy being a father. *He would be a good father, too.* If he would only let her help him get his life on track, do the proper thing for a man of his breeding. She repeated the old saw, "An apple doesn't fall far from the tree." Why was he so belligerent? He had his father's stubborn streak, but her backbone. That's why they clashed all the time. He had strength and determination. She admired that in a man. He wasn't weak like his father. She dozed off as the tranquilizer took effect.

Thirteen

Beatrice Ord was waiting in the study when the housekeeper brought Sean Cutcheon in. "Good morning Mr. Cutcheon, I'm glad you could come on such short notice," she said trying to sound cheerful for the housekeeper's sake.

The housekeeper brought in a tray with coffee and cookies. Mrs. Ord said "That will be all. I will call you if we need anything." She turned her attention to Sean Cutcheon, "It's Randy. I've gotten a letter from him. I want you to see if you can find out where he is. Apparently, he's married now and I want to know what this woman is all about."

"Do you have the name of the town?" Cutcheon asked.

Mrs. Ord handed him the slip of paper. "Its Los Montoyes, New Mexico. The letter was mailed three days ago from there. I sincerely doubt if he is there however. Perhaps you could find where he came from by checking gas stations, restaurants, etcetera along the major routes leading from the north. I suspect he is still in Colorado. He dearly loves Colorado. I doubt that he would leave it, especially not for New Mexico. He loves the winters," she said pacing as she spoke.

"I think your assumption is right. From what I learned before, he hung pretty close to home territory. I don't see him leaving the state. Does Ruth know anything?"

"No, no please don't involve her. She mustn't know about the letter that I received either. No one else should know. This is strictly between you and me." She handed Cutcheon a check. "This should cover your expenses for a time. Let me know, as soon as you can, whatever you come up with. Find that girl too. I have to know what she's up to." With that, she rang for the housekeeper. "Please show Mr. Cutcheon out," she said. "And thank-you for coming. I'll expect to hear from you in a day or two."

Beatrice Ord walked to the window and watched Cutcheon get in his car and head out the long driveway. Her mind followed him and the path he might take to discover where her son and her new grandchild might be. She hoped it wouldn't be long before she would be reunited with her son. "The prodigal son will come home," she said aloud. "They always do." She smiled to herself feeling hopeful about the future.

Fourteen

Danielle hammered relentlessly on JC's door. "JC, JC," she sobbed.

"Oh my god what happened, Danielle?" JC asked as she opened the door and saw Danielle.

"It's Randy JC, he went off the deep end. He started drinking again and he—" she cried uncontrollably. "—he said he invited a few people over to celebrate his new job. He said he was only going to have one drink. He—"

"Get in here, you poor thing," JC said looking up and down the street to see if Danielle had been followed. "I'm calling the police right now. I'll have that son-of—a gun put away for a good long time." JC said starting towards the telephone.

"No, wait JC, don't please." Danielle grabbed her friend's hand and pleaded with her.

"Danielle, he can't do this and get away with it. Look at you. Your eye is black and blue and almost swollen shut already. You're bleeding—your nose, and your mouth. Is anything broken? Are you okay? Should we get you to a doctor? Yes, we should call an ambulance."

"JC it's okay. I'm all right. I'm bruised that's all. I'll be fine. I just can't stay with him anymore."

"What about the baby? What if you lose the baby because of this?" JC asked.

"No, he only hit me in the head. The baby is fine. I'm fine. I hurt, but I'm fine. Can I please just stay with you tonight, JC?" she asked, holding her friend by the shoulders forcing her to look into her eyes.

"We've got to do something. Here let me get some ice. Then we are going to sit down and talk, girl. You are not going home to that monster, ever again. Do you hear me? This is the last straw. If you ever go back to him again, I'm done with you. Do you hear me?"

Danielle nodded her head. As JC pressed the icepack against her swollen cheek, she winced in pain. "Don't worry, JC, I have no intentions of ever going back to him. I have a child to think of now."

"That's the most sane thing I have ever heard you say," JC said putting her arm around Danielle. She took the washcloth she had brought and dabbed at the drying blood under Danielle's nose and lip. "Your lip is split pretty good. Do you think maybe you should have a doctor look at it?" she asked.

"No, it'll be alright I've had worse believe me."

"I'll go make up the guest bedroom for you, then we'll have some tea and figure out what you should do next. I still think you should turn him in. He deserves to pay for what he's done."

"When he gets sober he will realize what he's done. This baby means everything to him—he said so. He will regret what he's done."

"No, I don't mean regret. I mean he should pay. They should throw his ass in jail and throw away the key. That's what I mean. He should not get a token punishment. Some time in jail will let him see the light of day. He'd dry out then and not the easy Betty Ford clinic way either. He deserves to squirm," JC raved.

"Don't JC. Don't talk that way. It isn't like you to be so judgmental."

JC turned to Danielle and she could see the look of disbelief on her friend's face. "I understand how you feel, really I do Danielle, but why would you let yourself be a punching bag and then just let him get away with it? Is that your idea of punishment?" JC just stood facing Danielle, waiting for an answer.

Danielle burst into tears again. JC rushed to her side and held her.

"I'm sorry JC. I just can't do anything to hurt Randy; his family has hurt him enough. That's what this is all about, you know that. I've told you that."

"Okay. You handle it your way. Who am I to say what's right. I just know what I would do in your position. Or at least if it was me in your position."

"You can't be sure of what you would do until you live through it, JC. No one can be sure if love out weighs pain, or if pain is a part of loving. I don't know anymore. I only know as far as Randy is concerned, I want nothing more from him, for him, or punishment of any kind. At this point I'm just too numb to care."

"Okay, okay, we'll drop it until morning. How about a nice hot chocolate or maybe a cup of tea. It'll help you sleep. What do you say?" JC asked.

"I think tea would be nice. I'm really not tired yet." Danielle said following her friend to the kitchen.

Fifteen

Danielle cautiously opened the apartment door. She listened for sounds, snoring; anything to indicate Randy was there. She heard nothing so she edged her way into the stuffy apartment. Randy was gone; he didn't leave a note. The hot apartment smelled of sweat and stale beer. Danielle always hated the stifling heat trapped in the apartment by the glaring sun and the bakery below.

She pulled all the shades on the south and east sides and opened the windows half way. Cars rumbled by on the street below. A pigeon landed on the windowsill where she put the left over popcorn for him last night. She could smell garlic from the Italian restaurant across the street and she listened to roller blades rattling down the alley. Laughter scratched at her ego. She saw two women around her age loaded down with shopping bags. Their style reeked money. Instantly, she hated them. She pulled the shade down all the way, as if that would make them disappear. She cranked up the stereo to drown out the street noises.

Danielle opened a fresh pack of cigarettes, lit one, and took a long satisfying drag from it. Marlboro country she snickered. She tossed Randy's Playboy Magazine across the room and flopped down on the threadbare couch. In less than three hours, she'd be back listening to drunks at the Office Bar & Grill who solved everyone else's problems and talked to her like she was a thing rather than a person. God, how she hated them. She hated her life. She hated the world.

She thought about the fight she and Randy had last night.

"You're nothing but a cheap lay. As soon as I get on my feet I'm outta here" he had said.

She had called him everything but a white man and threatened to cut up his precious Harley.

"I'll kill you if you so much as look at the bike, you fucking bitch. You don't know when you're well off."

The fight ended as they always did—after he slammed her around .She had run off to JC's after he passed out.

"Trap, a god awful trap…I've dug my hole so deep I'll never get out," she mumbled aloud to the dank, still air. She crushed out her cigarette and went to the bathroom to take a shower and get dressed for work. If Randy showed up later, she would kick his ass out. She paid the rent. *He can just go find another sucker* she thought, flinging the towel over the shower door. Danielle scrubbed her body vigorously, trying to erase last night, a million last nights, vowing she'd make a new turn somehow. She *would* make a new turn. What she did not want was to end up like she remembered her mother so many years before.

Sixteen

Late at night, it always got to him. After everyone left and he was alone with his thoughts and the drugs and booze no longer kept his guilt and shame at bay. Drinking and smoking, while she worked and he partied because he couldn't live with himself anymore. Now, he had a wife and a child on the way. Now, he could no longer hide in the bottle. Where had it all started? His thoughts drifted back to another time.

She was such a gorgeous young thing when he met her that first day at the Office Bar. All pert and cute in her Dallas Cowboy type uniform. Brown hair, almost to her waist, not just brown but the color of warm moist earth, like the soil on my parents' farm. He didn't want to think of the farm or the estate or anything to do with that family. That family is the reason I am where I am. That wimp I call father, the domineering bitch that mother has become. When had everything changed? He couldn't remember. High school was full of sports, college bound classes, clubs and all the activities he could cram into a year. All of the four years he was at Blasedell Private High School, for the sickeningly rich, money had bought him many a favor, many a pay-off to keep his rebellious antics from spoiling his career. When he decided he didn't want to go into law school, that's when the trouble had started. He wanted metallurgical mining and engineering like his father. He wanted to keep up with the latest developments in mining and exploring. His mother had insisted that he become a lawyer because "every family needs a good corporate lawyer." Law was dull. Law was a cop out. He wanted hands on. He wanted to be by his father's side in a masculine business. He wanted a career, something that used brawn and brains.

That had nothing to do with Danielle. She would never know about this family if he had anything to say about it. I really do love that girl. I don't know why I go off half-cocked and slap her around. There is just so much on my mind. I really hate having her support me. I can't seem to keep it together. Every time I fill out a resume, it gets too complicated. They start checking and I get connected right back to that family. I can't tolerate it. Then mother sends one of her hired idiots out to find me to try to drag me home. When will it all end? Will it end before I lose that beautiful little lady that keeps hanging on to me though God knows why—I don't know why. Now the job starts next Monday. The past is history, I will see to that. He threw the half-empty beer bottle across the room. It landed with a crash against the refrigerator.

"Why can't I quit that shit?" he croaked.

The loud rap on the door startled Randy out of his half-conscious trip into the past.

"Yeah! Who is it?" He yelled back at the intrusion as he slipped the cassette tape that he'd been fondling between the cushions of the dingy couch. The door blew open, Shorty, and two of his thugs bolted through it. "What the hell? You don't have to bust the door down. I've been waiting for you to bring my money," Randy said trying to get up. The stocky slime-bag he knew as Mace slammed him back down on the couch. Shorty slid into the recliner directly across from him.

"We need to talk. Got sanctimonious all of a sudden, just because you are gonna be a daddy," Shorty said glaring at Randy.

He let the word "daaa-ddee" roll off his tongue in a whinny voice. Randy got a sick feeling in his stomach. He would like to close Shorty's smart mouth with a fist. Nevertheless, he knew he had better sit tight and let things go. He did not want to antagonize Shorty or his apes. Randy looked from Shorty to Mace, to Horse. As the name implied, Horse was as big as a horse and twice as ugly. He reminded Randy of a mule, all ears and brawn. Randy knew he was in trouble. How bad, he wasn't sure, but he did not plan to go out this way. Not now, when he had everything to live for. He started up from his seat again. This time Horse pushed him back and Mace grabbed one arm while Horse held him down. Randy had not seen Horse pull his gun from its holster, but he saw it now.

"Dear God help me," he shouted to his insides. "Don't let them do this. Not now." Randy struggled with every ounce of energy he could manage. "Why?"

Horse came down hard with the butt end of the pistol against the back of Randy's head. Randy slumped over on the couch.

"Drag him into the bedroom," Shorty growled at the two men. Shorty followed them. They laid him across the bed and took off his jeans shorts, the only clothes he wore in the stifling heat of the apartment. They arranged his body carefully on the bed. Mace pulled a syringe out of his pocket, uncapped it and let the cap drop to the floor. He pressed the plunger until two drops spurted from the needle and landed on Randy's arm. He inserted the needle into Randy's right arm and pushed the plunger all the way down. He wrapped the syringe in a handkerchief and put it back in his pocket.

Horse pulled the yellow-flowered sheet up over the body. Randy's chest heaved in and out, laboring for breath, and then he was still. Horse felt for a pulse. "He's gone," he said turning to Shorty.

"Let's get to hell to of here. Be sure anything you touched is clean. Don't want a scrap of evidence left behind. Horse, grab that fan from the living room and place it here in the bedroom doorway. He would have done that if he were going to bed in this heat. Hurry up before someone spots our car outside." Shorty picked up the matches beside the candle as though he was going to light it. He shook his head and replaced the matches on the nightstand.

The two men did as they were told. Shorty opened the door with his handkerchief and the men exited to the dimly lit hallway

At the bottom of the stairs, the three men stepped over the old homeless woman who appeared to be passed out drunk. Horse held the back door of the white Cadillac open for Shorty, shut it and then climbed in the passenger side of the front seat. Mace started the car and peeled out from the curb.

"Cool it, damn it. We don't want to draw attention to ourselves," Shorty barked at Mace.

Seventeen

Ruth Ord watched in the rear view mirror as the white Cadillac pulled up behind her. The park was deserted except for her sleek, silver Porsche and the white Cadillac. A short, rotund man in a blue linen suit with a blue-striped shirt and red tie squirmed out of the car. She recognized Shorty Delegano under the navy blue adventurer's hat. The man had taste in clothes anyway she mused. He approached the passenger side of the Porsche as two men got out of the Cadillac and stood outside leaning against the front doors surveying the park. Shorty slid into the passenger seat beside Ruth.

"It's done. Your thorn has been removed from your side, lady."

Ruth slung a bulging envelope at Shorty. He caught it and rifled through the bills. He let out a low whistle. "This will cover it, thanks. If you ever need another favor you know where to find me," he said grinning.

"I doubt that will be necessary. Just get out and leave me alone," Ruth growled at him.

"I'm gone, lady. Nice doing business with you." With that he slid out and he and the other two men got into the Cadillac and drove off.

Ruth waited until the red tail lights disappeared in the distance. She turned the key in the ignition and slammed the gas pedal to the floorboards. Tires squealed and the car lurched forward. She didn't let up on the gas until she was on the winding mountain road leading back to the Ord Estate. She wasn't sorry for what she had done. Randy had always been a thorn in her side. Her parents never noticed her when he was around. She was the one who had sacrificed her life to join in the family business. It was she who took care of things including her little brother when they would take their trips to Europe. It was she who would bail little brother out to keep the family name intact. It was always she. What thanks did she get? All her parents could both talk about was when Randy would eventually straighten himself out. When he finally gave them an heir to the Ord fortune, then all would be well in the world. Well, the world was all well now.

"How do you like those apples?" she screamed into the star-studded blackness of the Colorado sky.

Eighteen

Detective Sandy March was the first to arrive on the scene after the uniformed officer made the call that a body had been found in an apartment on Main Street. The coroner had been called but was not there yet.

"What do we have here?" March asked the officer that met him at the door.

"Looks like a guy died in his sleep. Landlady said his name is Randy Ord. No struggle, no signs of anything unusual...only..."

"Only what?"

"Well, the guys young, probably twenty-five years old or so. He seems to be in great shape. So how? Why did he just die? My gut tells me there's something wrong here."

"Okay," March said scanning the apartment. He knew an officer trained to notice and feel a scene usually had pretty good intuition, or gut reaction as the guys preferred to call it. He believed that the officer probably did sense something amiss. It would take further investigation to rule out foul play. He nodded toward the gray-haired lady sitting on the tattered living room sofa.

"This is the landlady, Mrs. Peoples," the uniformed officer said.

"Sorry to inconvenience you, Mrs. Peoples. However, we need to get your statement then you'll be free to go. I'm detective March, Durango PD."

"The trouble is a dead body in my apartment building. The trouble is not an inconvenience to me—it is total disaster. I—I—how will I ever be able to rent a place where someone has been murdered?" Her gaze darted around the room like she was an over-wound wind-up toy. She looked from March to the uniformed officer by the bedroom and back to March looking for either an answer or some consolation.

"No, trouble comes in buckets around here, not inconvenience," she said nervously. "I knew these two were no good. All the complaints about him beating up on the little lady. All the drinking and, I think from the trash that came in and out of here, there were drugs as well. I'll tell you anything I can."

March chose to ignore her assumption that it was murder for the moment. "How long have they lived here?"

"About six or eight months. I'd have to check my records to be sure. Actually, they looked like a nice enough couple then. I try to get good people in here. Those who seem down on their luck and need a reasonable place to rent. Good, honest folks. I can usually tell. However, not this time. Lord I never suspected someone would be killed here."

"We don't know that anyone was killed, Mrs. Peoples. It could be the guy's heart just quit on him. So, for now we're treating it as a death from natural causes. We do need to investigate. Simply routine, to rule out possible foul play. Do you know who his family is, where they are, or where the girl he was living with might be?"

"Don't know nothing about his family, but little Danielle works over on Durango Street at The Office Bar & Grill. Nobody's seen her around here for two or three days. Because I asked before I let myself into the apartment. Thought maybe they were just gone somewhere or maybe they moved out without telling me. That happens sometimes, people just leave without telling me; owing me back rent; leaving the place a filthy mess for me to clean up after them; no security deposit left for the cleaning either, but they do it, they do it. I did not want to just come in if they were still living here. Maybe she finally got smart and moved out on him," Mrs. Peoples said, shrugging her stooped shoulders. All the while she talked, she wrung her gnarled, arthritic hands.

"Okay. If you can come up with any of his or her friends' names, people who might have been around in the last week just give me a call. Here's my card. Thanks for your time. You are free to go now."

"I don't know none of their friends. I was never here when any of them were and no one here associated with them from what I could find out. Thanks, detective. That's all I need is a homicide to give my place a bad name. It's hard enough keeping this place low rent and letting young people live here. You know I could get a lot more for these rooms if I rented to older people."

Detective March ignored her play at being a philanthropist. He knew the history and the clientele that had rented here, the police had numerous calls to this building about loud parties, fights—people causing all sorts of trouble. This was a well-known trouble spot and Mrs. Peoples rented to anyone who came up with the money. The good ones complained about the maintenance and safety of the building, and were either evicted or moved out shortly. "I'm sure you could Mrs. Peoples. It's very kind of you to try to help the young folks. You be sure to call me if you think of any names."

"I will detective you can count on it."

The coroner was completing his examination of the body when Detective March approached the bedroom. "Any clues as to what happened?" he asked.

"Nothing in particular, not without an autopsy. There is one curious thing. There's two small burn marks next to this puncture mark on his right arm. There are no other tracks, so if he mainlined something, it's his first time. Not sure but it looks to me like a heroin burn. I will have to wait to get him back to the lab and do a toxicology test."

March nodded his head, looking at the blistered pockmarks leading to the tiny hole.

"Also, he has a bruise on the back of his skull. Not sure if it would have been enough to do him in, it doesn't look like it. I wouldn't even have spotted it with his long hair and all but when I rolled him over, his hair parted by what you would call a 'cowlick' and there it was. Won't know until we get him back to the morgue."

Sandy March looked around the cramped bedroom. "What side of the bed was he laying on?" he asked the coroner.

"Right here, on the left actually. Why?" he asked with a quizzical expression on his face.

March pointed to the jean shorts lying in a heap beside the right side of the bed. "What are his shorts doing over here then? Sure he could have crawled across the bed or gotten undressed and walked around the bed but it doesn't look as though he just stepped out of them. Suppose he could have just tossed them over there. What do you do with your clothes when you take them off, especially if you sleep in the buff?" he questioned the coroner.

"Well, I keep them close. You know, in case one of the kids gets up in the night or someone knocks on the door, that sort of thing."

"Exactly my point," March said. "Don't touch them until forensics gets here."

"Right. What did the landlady say about his family? We'll need their permission to do an autopsy you know. If he had one that is."

"Think the first thing I'll have to do is get hold of his girlfriend now. See what she can tell us. Has forensics been called?"

"The uniform said he called it in after he called you," the coroner said.

Detective March looked at the body on the bed. It had started to decompose already in the sweltering apartment. "Wonder what you'd tell me if you could talk now," March said as he lifted the blankets back to expose the naked body of a man too young to die in his sleep. Without the autopsy he couldn't be sure that statement was correct, but the guy seemed in decent physical shape. His thick brown, shoulder length hair framed the ghost white face. The square jaw was slack exposing a full set of straight, white teeth. A gold chain lay against the patch of brown hair on his chest.

Detective March's eyes followed the full length of his torso. It did look like he died peacefully in his sleep. No distinguishing marks other than the two tiny burn marks. A silver and turquoise Eagle ring on his right hand, a Seiko watch. A Seiko? How does a down and out unemployed stiff afford a Seiko? The proprietor said they lived from paycheck to paycheck. The bed was not messed, showed no signs of struggle or restless sleep. March noticed a small puddle of wax on the crate next to the bed that was obviously a makeshift nightstand. It looked as if a candle had been burning. It had burned itself out. The wax was mostly blue with a blotch of wine red. He could smell the faint hint of vanilla, and something else. He could not quite put his finger on the odor "Be sure forensics bags this wax," he said to the coroner's assistant; thinking perhaps that forensics might find what the other scent was, "and I want this matchbook dusted for finger prints too."

"Detective March, the forensic team is here." The uniformed officer said, motioning to the door.

"Great, have them get right to work. Get them to bag this wax and tell them I want a complete analysis of it. It has a smell I'm curious about. Also this book of matches. Be sure it gets fingerprinted."

"Will do," said the officer turning toward the door.

Detective March scanned the room taking in all the details. His instincts told him there was foul play. He did a rough sketch of the tiny room that was barely large enough for the double bed. The one dresser had only two drawers, gapping holes where the other drawers used to be showed a few pieces of women's clothes. A closet, with no door, was barren of clothes. Several empty hangers dangled on the closet pole. It seemed most of the occupant's clothes were in heaps on the floor. Not Mr. Neatness, he noted.

He scratched a few items in his notebook. There was an old newspaper on the nightstand next to the bed dated three days ago. So apparently, the guy could have been dead at least that long. No women's clothes were present anywhere else in the room. Odd, he thought, if he had a live-in girlfriend.

The forensic crew was busy dusting for fingerprints and combing through the heaps of clothes. "Be sure those shorts get to the lab," he said pointing at the single pair next to the bed. "And try not to get finger prints or other contaminants on them first."

"March, better have look here," one of the forensic team motioned to him. A black backpack and a black wooden box labeled cassettes lay open on the floor. There were college textbooks, a lab kit, metallurgical testing equipment and vials of chemicals all labeled very neatly. The box looked to be held together with gray duct tape. He read the labels on the vials. Cyanide—how interesting, he thought. What in the devil was he doing with cyanide in the closet?

"It was on the top shelf out of view of a casual observer. We should be able to get a lead on his family from these college textbooks. I'll call over there and try to get some information about our Randy Ord."

So, the body finally had a name and a connection. At least it seemed there was a connection to a school, perhaps a family. March hated John Doe's with no past or present—he was glad some life was showing up to biography the body.

"Check this out." The forensic investigator handed him a letter. "The man had a job interview with the Colorado Department of Mining & Exploration."

"See if he showed up for this interview. Never mind I'll check that out myself. Meantime keep digging. Be sure to check under the bed and any other nook or cranny for something that could open a door to this guy's life. Have someone look around outside, in garbage cans, you know, anywhere a perp could have dumped something. I don't think this guy died peacefully just because he died in bed."

"Wait a minute. Now I know why that name is familiar. Yes, Ord, Randy Ord. Why—okay, wait a minute—good grief, yes. Randolph Ord III. He has been working real hard at screwing up the family name. Don't remember how many DWI's and drunk and disorderly charges his family has fixed for him since high school. Shit. I don't want to have to tell them about this. It may just be the push that sticks Randolph Ord II into the grave. He has had one foot on a banana peel for a long time already."

Gordy Lesh, March's partner, wormed his way through the mingling of forensics team, coroner and ambulance crew to Detective March. "Sorry it took so long. I was taking the kids to the sitters and got stuck behind that blasted train," Lesh said apologetically. "What we got?"

"Not sure, looks like the guy died in his sleep. We don't know why yet. I was just on my way to try to find his live-in. Come on, I'll fill you in on the way over."

Detective March scanned the living room. He noticed the damaged plaster behind the door and the plaster dust on the floor. It appeared as though the doorknob had smashed into the wall very recently. He motioned to one of the forensic team members, "Check this out and be sure to note it in your report. Dust the knob, the frame and the door itself for fingerprints though with all the traffic in here any prints are probably gone."

"Looks fresh doesn't it?" the man said.

March nodded his head in agreement. He and Lesh threaded their way back out through the crowd of people. March told the officer in charge where he was going. They pushed through the gawkers in the hallway.

"Sepchak," he yelled at one of the uniformed officers, "get these people out of here. Put those who have seen anything in a separate room to talk to. Those who may have seen or heard something, get their statements. Have that room taped off now and make the rest of these people leave the vicinity."

He pushed his way to the front door. That was the trouble with small towns—everyone knew everyone else's business and any incident was cause for a gathering of the sidewalk superintendents and town gossips. The air was hot, dusty, but he felt a surge of relief from the stagnant air inside. There was a box fan going in the apartment, so why were the windows closed? He turned back to look at the dilapidated brick two-story. The paint was peeling off the window and door-trims, corners of brick and mortar eroded away by neglect and age. "What a dive," he mumbled half to himself.

"What?" Lesh questioned.

"Oh, nothing. That building is about ready to collapse around the tenants' ears and I can't say I'm sorry. That has been a headache for the PD since Mrs. Peoples took it over five years ago."

"That's a Roger," the young detective agreed.

"Danielle Maynard, the girl friend, works over at The Office Bar & Grill. We'll have her sign this authorization for a search of the apartment while we're there. Lets go see what she has to say. We'll walk. It's only a couple blocks away and I need to clean the stench of that apartment out of my nose," he said putting on his sunglasses against the intense Colorado sun.

Lesh grunted and fell in step with March's long-legged stride.

Two suits were sitting at the counter. They glanced over their shoulders briefly as Sandy March and Gordy Lesh entered the door of The Office Bar & Grill. A petite young woman was putting dishes away and wiping tables. She approached the men as they stood near the counter.

"Can I help you gentlemen," she said smiling.

"We need to speak with Danielle Maynard," Sergeant March said to the girl.

"That would be me," Danielle said feeling an ominous heaviness in the air. She tried to calm herself, tried to tell herself to act normal. What in the hell was normal anyway? She wasn't sure anymore. "Except the last name is Ord now."

"Is there some place we could talk in private?" March asked.

"Ah, sure. Just a minute while I ask JC to cover for me." Why did she think Randy was dead? She could feel it. She hadn't seen him in days. What did these cops want? She was sure she'd find out soon enough. Maybe Randy was in some sort of trouble again. "Those damn drugs, " she cursed silently.

March noticed the display of candles sitting on the far end of the counter. A sign above them said "Candles To Die For by Danielle Maynard." There were little price tags attached to the plastic wrap that covered each. A bow in a matching or contrasting color sealed each candle. *Interesting.* March made a mental note of the display.

"Gentlemen, if you will follow me," she said as she led the two men into the cramped office at the rear of the restaurant. "Please have a seat. What is it you want to talk to me about?"

"I'm afraid we have some bad news about your boyfriend, or do I mean husband?" March corrected himself.

"What, what about Randy, and he's my husband, not boyfriend. Is he hurt? Is he in some kind of trouble?" She felt herself start to shake all over. It wasn't shock but it could have been. The revelation that he had been found dead, she knew, was next. She didn't know why or how she knew this. She only knew it was true. She did not know what she should do or say.

"Sorry, I didn't know he was your husband. The landlady said he was your boyfriend."

"Just tell me what's going on. What has happened? Where is Randy?" she asked on the verge of tears.

"I'm afraid there's no easy way to say this, Ms. Maynard, I mean Ms. Ord. He's dead."

Danielle collapsed. Involuntarily her knees just gave way. The next thing she knew, the two men were lifting her to the chair behind the desk. "I'm sorry," she mumbled. Tears began to stream down her face. "How? What? Where? When?" The questions poured out of her mouth. She had a hard time believing it was true. Up until now, it had all seemed like a bad dream that would never come true. She had wished him dead a thousand times.

"We really do not have any details yet, Ms Ord," March said with his hand on her shoulder "Gordy, go get the lady a glass of water, or would you prefer something stronger?" he said turning to Danielle.

"Water's fine, I-I don't drink," she stammered reaching for a tissue from the box on the desk. "Where did they find him?" She asked finally getting up the strength to try to find out what they knew or suspected.

"He was in bed. The landlady came to collect the rent. When there was no answer, she let herself in and found the body."

"How did he die?"

"We don't know. It appears he just died in his sleep. There doesn't seem to be any evidence of foul play. "

"I told him to quit drinking or he was going to kill himself. I told him he needed help, but he wouldn't listen."

"I'm truly sorry, Ms. Ord. Does he have any family that we should contact?" March knew he did, but he was fishing, always the detective.

"His family lives over in Colorado Springs. He hasn't had anything to do with them in years. I only found out about them myself a little while back. Yes, they need to be told. It'll be a terrible blow to his father. I will contact them myself. If that's okay. It is going to be such a shock. I do not know if his father can stand the shock. It would be better coming from me." Her words stuccatoed and her head swiveled, she knew she was talking but the words seemed foreign, in a voice not her own.

The walls of the small room seemed to be closing in on her, squeezing the breath out of her. She felt the urge to bolt out the door and never stop running. Danielle didn't want the detective to know that Randy hadn't told her about his family. She didn't want them to know about the sister's visit, or the arrangement they wanted to make with her when they heard she was pregnant and that she planned to leave Randy. She didn't want them to know that the sister refused to give Randy the money to go for alcohol treatment because she thought he would blow it on drugs instead. These inconsequential thoughts screamed in her head.

"All right ma'am if you think that would be best."

Danielle's face was so white March thought she was going to pass out again. She looked like someone had drained all the color from her skin. March handed her the glass of water Lesh had brought. "Ah, one other thing, ma'am. We need you to sign this form so we can complete our investigation of the scene in case Mr. Ord did not die in his sleep of natural causes. Other wise we'll need to get a search warrant, that involves a lot of hassle we'd rather not have to do."

Danielle reached for the pen he handed her. She was in a daze, his words not quite registering; she felt the room growing close. Again she felt like she was suffocating.

"Is everything okay?"

They all turned to see JC in the doorway.

"Oh, JC," Danielle cried holding out her arms, "Randy's dead." The tears started in earnest then. Danielle couldn't help herself. It was finally over and she was coming unglued. Control, she told herself, control. Don't lose it now.

"God, Danielle, how?" JC gushed as she hurried to her friend's side, her face twisted in sympathy with Danielle's pain.

"We aren't sure, ma'am. Looks like he died in his sleep. Until the autopsy, we won't know. Since you're next of kin, Ms. Ord, we need you to identify the body and to okay an autopsy. Do you think you can do that?"

"Can't you see she's shattered? Can't this wait, let her collect herself a little?" JC held Danielle to her, scowling at the two officers.

"It can wait until morning," March said. "We do need to try to get some answers and the body has started to decompose pretty badly considering the heat." He had no sooner said it then he regretted it. He did not need to say the body was decomposing. "Ah, the sooner we can do the autopsy the better our chances of finding out what really happened. I need to ask, Ms. Ord, when was the last time you saw your husband alive?"

" I-I don't know. Three, maybe four days ago," she said through the sobs, swiping at her tears with a tissue. "He stopped here for coffee, but I didn't have time to talk to him, we were too busy. I don't want him cut up. Isn't it bad enough that he's dead—why does he have to be cut up, too?" Danielle cried hysterically, pushing away from her friend's grasp.

"Coroner needs to list a cause of death ma'am," Lesh interjected. "Anytime there is an untimely death, the medical examiner has to fill out a report. He can't do that without knowing the cause of death. And in this case there needs to be an autopsy to determine that."

"Look officers, I'll get her down there first thing tomorrow morning. We'll discuss the possibilities of an autopsy then. Now, I would appreciate it if you would just leave us alone."

"I understand," said March turning to leave. "When did you see him last, miss?"

"The same day Danielle saw him. I didn't talk to him either, just gave him coffee. He sat in a booth by himself and left about 15 minutes after he came in. He never did like crowds, and we were very busy that day as Danielle said." JC led them out of the tiny office into the café.

"See you tomorrow then. And we'll need to talk to you too, JC. Is that the name you go by?"

"Yes, Jeryl Catherine Smythe, JC to everyone though. I'm afraid I don't know much of anything," she said leading them out the office door and through the restaurant. "I know he beat the crap out of her a few times, but she still loved the guy. God only knows why. "

"Where did you meet her?" Lesh asked.

"When she applied for a job here. We work together everyday. We became good friends."

"Have you talked with Mr. Ord at all? Got his side of the story? Found out what made him tick?"

"No, I haven't. I'm Danielle's friend, not that creep's. I told her to dump him months ago. What does she do? She turns up pregnant and marries the jerk. Go figure. Now I have work to do and a friend to take care of. Please leave," she said abruptly opening the door and ushering them out.

"See you tomorrow then," March said. "Oh, one more thing Ms—ah, JC, there seems to have been a party at the apartment. Any chance you could get us a list of Randy's friends who may have been there?"

"Yeah, sure. I'll ask Danielle to make one up for you. We'll give it to you tomorrow. I think she's too upset to do it right now," JC said.

Looking back through the door, March saw Danielle crumpled in a heap at the desk where they had left her. Her body heaving as she sobbed. March longed to hold her, try to comfort her. She looked so fragile and young.

"What's with you, March? That girl really got to you, didn't she? It's written all over your sorry face. Jeez man, you know better than that. Snap out of it," Lesh taunted him.

"Mind your own business. Can't a guy feel sorry for someone without you making a federal case out of it?" March said, walking briskly along Durango Street back to where they had left the car parked. Lesh's stubby legs double-stepped with every stride March made, as he tried to keep up with his partner.

Nineteen

What if they find out? What if they think I killed him? No, she reassured herself, they couldn't. The candle is still there. I didn't light it. I will go back and get it, and, oh God! and that cyanide literature. She heard the short worried bursts of the Silverton Narrow Gauge nearing the Main Street crossing. It seemed to shout, "go, go-o, go, go-o." She flung her apron on the desk and darted for the door.

"Danielle, Danielle, wait," JC raced after her friend but stopped outside the door. She could not leave the restaurant. "Danielle," she screamed in a desperate attempt to stop her friend.

"I'll be all right," Danielle yelled over her shoulder as she tore down the street. Her mind focusing on the thin air she sucked into her lungs. She had to get that evidence out of the apartment.

She stopped in the alley behind the building. The squad car and ambulance were pulling away from the curb. She scanned the street. The detectives would have a plain car; she hesitated, trying to determine if the vehicles parked across the street were shoppers or unmarked police cars. Her breath seemed to leap out of her open mouth in loud bursts. She leaned over, grasped her knees, and inhaled slowly and deeply. Out of shape, still not used to this thin air, she told herself. She leaned into the wall to brace herself then slid down the wall, squatting behind some cardboard boxes to wait until she could be sure the apartment was empty.

Panic held her heart hostage refusing to let it beat normally. She waited until street noises quieted and onlookers disappeared to continue their speculation and lives elsewhere. Cautiously, she uncurled and stood up. When she saw no one in the street, she darted into the stairwell and listened. Everything seemed normal. She could hear the familiar business of the bakery below and Mrs. Ellis' TV blaring "Young and the Restless." Danielle felt the horror of what she had almost done. She became too frightened to go up. She dashed back to the alley and the protection of the boxes. She replayed the scene from several nights ago in her mind. The night she had come home to light the candle and snuff Randy out of her life once and for all. She huddled among the boxes waiting for the safety of darkness. Her mind replayed the scene as if it were happening all over again.

She was back crawling under the blankets in the spare bed she was using at JC's apartment. A cold sweat ran icy chills down her back. She was glad JC didn't hear her come in. She wouldn't want to have to explain where she had been at this hour in the morning. She bundled the blankets around her and closed her eyes. Oh, how she wished it were Randy's arms holding her in the eons before trouble started in their relationship. She could see him lying there so peacefully sleeping. He hadn't budged when she entered the bedroom to light her special candle. She had looked at him thinking how peaceful he looked without a care in the world, nothing frightening to disturb him.

His son, his heir to the Ord fortune would never know his father. That thought caused tears to well in her eyes. But, she couldn't light the candle and had backed quietly out of the room, being careful not to trip on the fan Randy always put in the doorway to cool the bedroom in the steaming upstairs apartment. He was a wonderful man, deep down, but he had turned into an animal. She couldn't trust his mood from one minute to the next. She never knew if he was going to lash out in anger or make passionate love to her. She couldn't get away from him and she couldn't stay with him any longer. Quietly she closed the door behind her and made her way down the narrow hallway and dimly lit stairs out to the street.

She stepped quietly around the old homeless woman asleep in the doorway. "Poor woman," she had breathed dropping a five-dollar bill into the woman's bag. "At least I have JC and a place to lay my head at night," she whispered as she felt the cool freshness of the Colorado night against her skin. Gingerly Danielle had made her way outside and hit the alley running. She didn't stop until she was safely inside JC's apartment.

Only then did the reality of what she had planned to do hit her. Tears poured from her sleepless eyes. She mourned the near loss of the only man she had dared to love. She mourned the near loss of the father her unborn child would grow up without. Finally fitful and nightmare-filled sleep came; the tear-soaked pillow would forever be the only witness to her feelings of quiet desperation. That was then. Now she must face the reality of Randy's death and hope she was not somehow implicated in it.

Content that all the police had left the building, she cautiously climbed the stairs plastering herself to the wall, reading the graffiti as she went. Nervously she fought her key into the scarred ancient lock on the door and quietly slid under the yellow police tape and inside. The smell of death lingered in the stale air. She heard footsteps in the hallway. Holding her breath, she stood motionless. Heavy footsteps lumbered down the hall, pausing at her door and then moved on.

Someone knocked on a door down the hall. She listened to the knocking again, then the heavy footsteps coming back toward her apartment. The rap on her own door caused the hairs on her neck to rise. Sure that whoever it was could hear her heart pounding and her labored breath, she stood motionless. The clumsy footsteps proceeded down the hall and clump-clumped down the stairs. Danielle collapsed on the couch, closing her eyes. Her legs felt like five-ton logs, her spine like Jell-O, as she forced air deeply into her lungs. Get it together, she told herself. She pulled her reluctant body upright and went to the bedroom to get the candle from the nightstand where she had left it.

It was gone! Tiny dried drips of wax puddled in the saucer where the holder had been. Panic seized her, her eyes wildly scanning the room. The candle was gone and worse, the puddled wax told her it had been burned.

She spun around and raced out of the apartment, down the stairs and out the door, her mind reeling with fear. They had the candle or what was left of it, but who had burned it? Why? Did Randy wake up and light it? She ducked back into the alley trying to decide what she should do next. She'd go to JC's, pack her stuff and run. Get on the first bus and just keep going. It was the only way. She had a little money saved, enough to get her away from here. She'd work her way back to Wisconsin and her Aunt Mary's farm. They'd never find her. *I didn't light the candle. I'm not responsible for Randy's death.* She clutched her belly cradling Randy's child and collapsed in a heap among the boxes in the alley, crying all the tears she'd ever saved from all the pain she had ever borne.

It was the black dark of late night when she finally pulled herself up and threaded her way down the back alleys to JC's apartment.

Twenty

Danielle held on to JC's arm like she was clinging to a life boat in a turbulent sea as Detective Sandy March lead them down the long sterile hallway and to a window that looked into a room lined with locker like compartments. The coroner stopped at one and slid open a drawer. A body was covered by a sheet. He wheeled the gurney close to the window and uncovered the corpse, exposing a ghostly, ash-gray face. Danielle felt her knees give way. March caught her and she melted against him. She turned her face away from the ghastly scene, sure she was going to throw up.

"I'm truly sorry Ms. Ord. Is it Randy Ord?"

"Yes, yes. I think I am going to be sick. I need air," she said pushing past March and rushing to the door. JC followed her out. Danielle leaned against the cold sterile wall, her gut tied in knots, and the room swirled before her. When she closed her eyes, all she could see was Randy's puffy ash-gray face before her. She raced down the hall not knowing where she was going. She needed to get outside. She needed the fresh brisk air of the Colorado mountains.

"Danielle, wait," JC called to her.

March rushed past JC and caught up with Danielle. "Wait, let me—"

Danielle pushed him away and fled through the doors to the street. She collapsed on the park bench under a huge ash tree beside the walkway. Tears streamed from her eyes and she began retching. JC was beside her suddenly, holding her.

"Oh God! Oh God! JC, I never really wanted him dead. I just wanted him the way he used to be. It's my fault. I wished he would die. I was even ready to kill him myself."

"Hush, hush," JC soothed Danielle against her shoulder. "Don't blame yourself. He was a louse; he got exactly what he deserved. Your wishing did not cause his death. He deserved to die."

"I'm really sorry about this," March said cautiously approaching the two women. "I do need your permission to do an autopsy, Ms. Ord. Just a couple papers to sign in my office. We can get this unpleasantness all over with." He reached for her arm. JC slapped at his hand.

"Leave her alone, let her get some air," she snapped.

"Look, I know this is unpleasant but we need to get it over with. Okay? I will give you a few minutes, then please bring her back inside. My office is on the second floor. The receptionist will show you where."

"In a few minutes," Danielle managed to whisper.

March gazed at her for a long moment, turned on his heel, and walked back inside.

"Its okay, JC, lets get this over with. If they need a lousy autopsy I'll sign their stupid papers." Danielle turned and took JC's hand as they walked back into the old stone building.

March stood up as the women entered. "Thanks, and I'm sorry about all this," he said motioning to the two chairs across the desk from him.

Danielle and JC settled into the seats.

"Would you like something to drink? Coffee, a soda, anything?" he asked apologetically.

"No, nothing, thanks," Danielle said. JC nodded in agreement. "Let's just get this over with."

"Please sign here where I've checked," March said turning the paper toward her and handing her a pen.

He retrieved the papers as she signed them. "About that list you were going to make up for me. Did you have time?" he questioned.

"Yes." Danielle reached into her purse and produced a folded piece of paper. "These are the regulars. There may have been others. I'd have no way of knowing as I haven't been around in a week."

"That's okay. We will get any additional names from these people as we talk to them. Thanks for your cooperation. You are free to go now and thanks again for coming down. I know this is a bad time for you. We'll let you know as soon as we can when the body can be released for burial."

March watched as the two women left. Something nagged at him about JC. He could not put a finger on it. Maybe it was just her attitude. She did not seem to be telling all she knew. He had no proof of that, just a gut reaction. He had an uncanny way of reading people and he was usually right. He did not want to be right this time, but he felt one of those women knew why Randy Ord was laying on a slab in the morgue. He gathered up the papers and took them downstairs.

"Get me a report on this man as soon as you can will you doc?" March said to the gray-haired man in a surgical gown.

"I'll get right on it, Mr. March. Coroner puts the time of death about three maybe four days ago, so it maybe a little tough to get too much information right away, but I'll do my best. Should have the initial report on your desk tomorrow morning."

"Thanks," March said as he turned and left the room.

Twenty-one

March and Lesh climbed the concrete steps of the old Grey Elephant apartment complex where Horn, and several of Randy's friends bunked. Lesh looked at the row of mailboxes at the foot of the wooden stairs. "No one named Horn listed here," he said.

"I'm not surprised." March said. "Guess we could start knocking on doors. Somebody probably knows which dump he crashes in."

The numbers were missing on most of the apartment doors; graffiti sprawled the length of the hallway and up the wall and on the stairs. From X-rated language to phone numbers, it was all there, a regular directory of twentieth century culture on the lower side of life.

Lesh knocked on the door where March had stopped. Loud music cut through and mingled with other sounds from within the paper-thin walls.

"Who the hell do you want?" an angry voice bellowed from the other side.

"We're looking for Horn. Is he around?" March shouted back, knowing a whisper could probably carry if not for the music blasting some unrecognizable language on the other side.

"Who wants him?" the voice yelled back.

"Durango PD. It's about a friend of his."

"He ain't got no friends. Anyway he ain't here." The door opened a crack and a bearded Neanderthal with swollen eyes peered out.

"Do you know when he'll be back, or where he's gone? We just want to ask him a few questions about Randy Ord, nothing serious," March said.

"Horn don't live here any more. We took the place over. He moved over on Ash Street, 504 Ash Street. What about Randy? He in some kind of trouble?" Neanderthal asked.

"Who am I talking to?" March asked back.

"People call me K-9 or Dog. I hang with Randy sometimes. Is he in trouble, man?"

"Not exactly. We found him dead this morning and want to find out if any one had seen him or was with him in the last week or so."

The door opened the rest of the way and the man staggered back into the chaotic mix of furniture and bodies sleeping in the large living room.

"Damn, man. I was at his party last Friday night, but hell, I been too sick to get out of bed since then. Hey Thelma, you or Mixer see Randy since the party?"

Voices in the background confirmed that no one had been in touch with Randy since the party.

"Do you know anyone else who was at the party that might know what happened with him between then and now?" Lesh asked stepping from behind March.

"Nah, hell no. We were all there. Val, Mixer, Thelma, Horn, me—Wait, Shorty was here, too. He's got a place over on Colorado Avenue. Hey, anyone know Shorty's address?" He yelled behind him to the group behind the door.

No one seemed to know where Shorty lived. March and Lesh turned to leave when a man came through the front door to the apartment building. His gray leisure suit was open, showing a red shirt and a bulge under his left arm. He quickly tried to button the jacket to cover the bulge.

"Hope you've got a permit for that," March said pointing to the man's left arm.

"You think I'm nuts? Of course I do," he snarled back at them.

"Mind telling us your name? Durango PD. I'm detective Sandy March and this is my partner, Gordy Lesh," March said flashing his badge.

"Go by the name of Jimmy Delegano. I carry this thing for protection when I have to come into these seedy places to collect the rent. Some of these guys don't part easily with their money and they'd as soon take it back as let me walk out with it."

"We were looking for you," Lesh said.

"Me? Why? Hey, man, I'm clean. Ain't never done nothing illegal around here." He turned as red as his shirt.

"It's really not about you," March said. "It's about Randy Ord. We understand you were at his party Friday night. Have you seen him since then?"

"Ah, no," he hesitated scratching his head. "No, I went home and been working at the Little Italian Restaurant every day since. Don't usually see Randy more than once or twice a month at the most. Why? Is he in some kind of trouble?"

"We found his body in his apartment." Lesh said, "Can you tell us anything about that?"

"Where? Did someone shoot him or what?" Shorty asked, visibly agitated.

"Looks like he died in his sleep," March said.

"Oh, that's too bad. Sorry I can't tell you a thing. Haven't seen him since the party. Now look if that's all the questions, I have a job to do here and time is money." He held out his hand to March.

"Guess that's all for now, but if you think of anything, anything at all, give us a call, will you?" Of course, March knew he wouldn't have any more to do with cops then he absolutely had to. He did not expect to hear from him again any time soon.

As they carefully picked their way between children and toys and older women catching up on neighborhood gossip on the concrete steps outside, March wondered about Shorty and how he fit with Randy's crowd.

"How do you figure that guy would be at a party with Randy and his cronies unless it was to deliver the party goods?" Lesh voiced March very thoughts. "Think we should check our records, see what we can dig up on our Mr. Delegano."

"Next stop, Dolby and his main squeeze, so the list says," Lesh said looking at the note pad he carried. "Over on LaPlatta".

Dolby opened the door dressed in a pair of ragged, faded jeans, his blonde hair looked like a squirrel nest, dark circles under his blue eyes lined in red veins.

"If he ain't careful he could bleed to death through his eyes," Gordy Lesh mumbled under his breath.

"Good morning. Are you Dolby Lewis?" Detective March asked.

"Depends on who wants to know," the man grumbled in a raspy voice that reminded March of a rock singer who had screamed himself voiceless.

"I'm Sergeant March and this is my partner Gordy Lesh. We're with the Durango PD. Can we come in? We need to talk to you."

"What about? I ain't done nothing. Me an the old lady may party hardy but we keep our noses clean."

"Actually it's about a friend of yours. Randy Ord."

"Randy in some kind of trouble officer?" Dolby asked rubbing his eyes.

"No, actually he was found dead yesterday morning," Lesh said.

"Shit! Oh, shit, man." Dolby was obviously upset; he raked his hands through his blonde mop, turning around and back. He staggered back into the room, "Skeet, Skeet. Woman get your ass out here. There's a couple of cops at the door. Randy's dead, man. Randy's gone."

A redhead wrapping herself in a flimsy shell of a duster swaggered out of what March assumed was the bedroom. She pulled at her hair trying to get it out of her eyes.

"What did you say? Randy, something happened to Randy? Is Danielle all right? Did somebody kill him or what?"

Her high-pitched voice was like fingernails on a chalkboard to March. "No, ma'am, we didn't say anyone killed him. We just said he was found dead in his bed at the apartment he and Danielle used to share."

"What do you mean used to? Those two just got married a couple months ago. They are thick as thieves. He loves his old woman," Dolby rasped at the detectives.

March was not about to update them on the state of the Ord's relationship. "When did you see him last?" he asked.

"Last Friday night we had a party over there." He grinned broadly, showing the few grimy brown teeth he had left. "Randy always could throw one hell of a party."

Skeet sat on the threadbare couch her head in her hands. "How could this happen? Randy can't be a day over thirty. Thirty-year olds don't just die in their sleep."

"That is exactly what I thought Ms., ah...er, Skeet. That's why I need to question anyone who has any information on

Randy and what he did last week or the week before," March said aiming his question at Skeet.

"Randy just got back the day he threw the party. He had been up in Denver. Some part-time job thing, I guess." Dolby offered.

"Did he tell you why he went up there?" Lesh asked.

"No, didn't know he was gone until he came back actually. All he said was he had a job, some guy from some trucking outfit hired him right out of the blue."

"That's all he said? Are you sure?" March persisted.

"That's it, man. Got no reason to lie. I don't know shit about where he was or what he did. That's the God's honest truth."

Skeet nodded her head in agreement. "Danielle wasn't at the party, but she works nights so no one thought anything of it. She usually sits in her little room playing with her candles anyway when she is there. She doesn't have nothing to do with the rest of us. Can't understand how her and Randy stayed together. They don't seem to have nothing in common." Her voice modulated up and down like a siren. March could not wait to get away from her voice.

"Well, guess that's all the questions I have at this time. If you think of anything you've forgotten about, call me downtown."

"When's his funeral? Do you know anything about arrangements?" Dolby asked as he held the door for the detectives.

"We're doing the autopsy first. Then he'll be released to next of kin, be that his family or his wife. You'll have to contact one of them. "

"Wait a minute, what family? He didn't have any family. Told me they all died in a terrible automobile accident when he was in some college." Dolby's face twisted in surprise.

"Apparently, that's not true. Maybe you should get a hold of Ms. Maynard, I mean Mrs. Ord and ask her about details."

The door shut quietly behind them as the two men picked their way down the hallway strewn with papers and garbage.

"Can you believe people live like this?" Lesh asked. "Where's the health officer? What is the landlord doing, or who is he paying to look the other way about this dive?

The fresh air of the street welcomed them once more. March turned to Lesh and said, "Randy Ord seems to be one big puzzle. Even the people who knew him don't or didn't know him. I'm not sure what to make of this guy. Why would someone whose family is worth millions abandon that life for one of drinking, drugs and batting the love of his life around like a ping-pong ball? It just doesn't wash."

"The human animal," Lesh said shaking his head. "Who's next?"

"While we're on this side of town we may as well look in on his buddy Horn, ah, James Darton, the paper work says, but everyone calls him Horn. Big nose says the people who know. Always horning in where he doesn't belong."

"Sounds like a nice guy," Lesh said getting into the passenger side of the blue sedan.

No one was home at the address on Ash Street when March and Lesh arrived. They headed back to the police station ready to call it a day. It had been a long one and March's head ached with unanswered questions and suspicions. He needed that autopsy report. He was sure it would reveal something.

The Silverton Durango Narrow Gauge Train squeaked across their path. The whistle moaned its approach through town to the depot. Cameras and tourists lined the windows.

"Love the sound of that train," March said. "Always sounds so sad, like the old west movies."

Lesh nodded as they waited for the train to get through the crossing. "I'm going to check with the lab and see if they have turned up anything concrete with the stuff that they got at Randy Ord's apartment. You might as well get your paperwork done and go home for the day," March said.

With the list in hand, Marsh and his partner checked off the names they had already interviewed from the list they had found in the address book beside the phone in the apartment.

"Let's run on over to the Colorado Basin Mining and Engineering Company to see what we can dig up there. That's where Mr. Ord had his interview," March said.

Twenty-two

"Look Mother, I tried to find him. Instead, I found the cheap little slut he is living with."

"No, wait, Ruth. He's married. He said he has a child on the way." Beatrice Ord went to her desk and took out the letter she had received from Randy. She handed it to Ruth. "I got this a couple weeks ago," she said sitting down on the desk chair. "I hired a private detective to try to track him down. He came up with a seedy character Randy's been working for, but so far no lead on that guy."

Ruth was stunned silent for a long moment while her mind raced to all sorts of dark corners. What "seedy character"? Was it Shorty Delegano? And would it tie her to him if he found him? The same man she had found connected to Randy. Could the PI know? What did he know? She had to stop this investigation now before it was too late.

"Call off your dogs, Mother. I know where Randy is or at least where his wife is. I'll go to him, tell him Daddy is sick. I'm sure he'll come home. No need to waste your money or time on sleaze bag private eye."

Beatrice Ord glared up at Ruth. "Why have you been hiding this from me? How did you find out where he was?" Rage blushed red from the lace neckline of the white blouse peaking out of a tailored suit to the perfectly coiffed gray hair. Gray-green eyes beaded into stiletto darts that riveted Ruth to the spot.

"Mother, wait. Don't blame me. Why do you always blame me for everything? Your son has been on the wrong path for years. Why can't you just let him live or destroy his life the way he chooses? I'll go talk to your precious baby for Daddy's sake, but, don't you blame me if he runs for cover again." She spit the words at Beatrice Ord.

"Wait Ruth, wait. Simmer down a minute. Let's talk this through. Your father is the important one now. Let's-let's think this through."

Ruth didn't want to parry with her mother any more. She needed to get away from her dominance to think, to do her own planning. She felt trapped. She needed to find out what the PI knew.

"Okay mother but I won't listen to any more bullshit about precious Randy. Who is this private Dick that you have got hot on his trail and—"

Her speech was interrupted by the telephone. Beatrice snatched up the receiver like it was on fire, glad to be done with her daughter's tirade for the length of a phone call at least.

"Hello," her controlled and dignified voice cooed into the phone. "This is she. Who? Who did you say this is?"

Ruth watched as her mother's face emptied of color and she slumped back into her chair.

"Yes, Danielle, how are you dear?" Sugar dripped from her words like maple sap during spring. Ruth felt like vomiting.

"Oh, my God, no! When? How? Are you sure?" Beatrice Ord was motioning to Ruth to come near her. She clutched Ruth in a grip that cut the circulation in Ruth's hand. "Randy's dead, this is his wife on the phone," she said covering the mouthpiece. She handed the telephone to Ruth, "I-I can't," she stammered as tears formed and she started shaking, losing the control that was her fortress.

Ruth took the telephone from her mother and listened while Danielle explained what she knew. Gently she hung up the phone and put her arms around her mother's shoulders. "I'm sorry Mother," she said.

"Who will tell your father? It will kill him," Beatrice said trying to regain her composure.

"We'll tell him together Mother. Give yourself a bit to get over this yourself."

"The funeral—the arrangements. We will have to—"

"Hold on a minute, Mother. They won't release Randy's body until the autopsy is done. We have plenty of time. I'm going to call Dr. Mansfield. You need to have him here with you now." She released her hold on her mother and rang for the housekeeper as she dialed Dr. Mansfield's number.

Twenty-three

March and Lesh entered the spacious office. Mahogany and teakwood emitted a wood and polish smell.

"Please come in. May I offer you a drink?" Mr. McCallister asked, motioning to the black leather sofa as he walked toward the fully stocked bar. A picture window and a massive bookcase completed the décor.

"No, thanks. We're on duty," March said. "We wanted to ask you a few questions concerning a potential employee. Apparently, you had set up an appointment to interview a Randolph Ord III some time last week. Is that true?"

"Randolph Ord, hmm. Oh yes, I remember. Nice young man, early thirties, sort of down on his luck. Yes, he came in. Matter of fact he is supposed to start a week from last Monday. What do you need to know?"

"Well, I'm afraid Mr. Ord won't be coming in. We found him dead in his apartment yesterday. We wanted to know if he actually turned up for the interview and what the results were."

"I'm sorry to hear that. His credentials were of the highest caliber. He graduated *suma cum laude*. The background check we did on him indicated he came from a reputable family. His physical was good. I was looking forward to having him on board. What a shame. Any idea what happened?"

"Not at this point. It appears he died in his sleep. Who was the doctor that did his physical?"

"Just a minute. Ms. Hastings, would you pull the file on Randolph Ord? He would be a new employee," he said into the intercom. An older woman appeared moments later with a file and handed it to Mr. McCallister. "Let's see that would have been a Doctor Ishling, over at Bay Shore Medical Clinic. He does most of our pre-employment physicals. He's very thorough."

"Thanks," March said standing to leave. "We won't take any more of your time."

"Well, he did have a future," Lesh said as they got back into the blue sedan and fished their way back into traffic headed for the Bay Shore Medical Clinic.

"I suppose we could just call Dr. Ishling. But, I really prefer a face-to-face. Sometimes body language and the vibes you get from a person tell you a lot more than just a voice over the phone." March knitted his eyebrows in thought. "Why would a thirty-year old man in excellent physical condition up and die in his sleep?" he asked as much to himself as to Lesh.

"Good question. But, you know how many supposedly healthy high school athletes have bit the dust lately," Lesh answered.

"True enough, but that's either on the game field or court during the heat of a game. This guy was lying in his bed. Do you think he could have drunk himself to death? I mean it's not unheard of."

"Hardly. From what we've heard, he's used to party time. His system has been overloaded many a time. No, had to be something else. Maybe his heart just gave out," Lesh said.

~ * ~

"Glad you could see us on such short notice Dr. Ishling," March said taking a chair opposite the doctor.

"I was about to grab a cup of coffee anyway. What can I do for you gentlemen?" he asked, curiosity written all over his face.

"We need to know what you can tell us about a Randolph Ord III. He came to you for a pre-employment physical last week. He was to go to work for the Colorado Basin Mining and Engineering Company. They gave us your name."

"I'll have to check the records. I see so many patients on a one-time basis it's hard to keep track of them. It will only take a couple minutes. Jane, get me the file on Colorado Basin would you please?" he said to the nurse at the desk.

He flipped through the file. "Here, looks like Randolph Ord was in fine shape. No problems that I turned up. He smoked, drank a little bit too much sometimes but otherwise he didn't seem to have any problems."

"Thanks Doctor."

"No problem. Anything else I can do let me know. If I can be so bold as to ask, is there some hang-up with our Mr. Ord?"

"He was found dead in his apartment yesterday."

"No, that man was in excellent condition. What does the autopsy show?" Dr. Ishling asked.

"We're still waiting for results. I thought it was rather funny myself. From looking at him, he seemed healthy enough. Guess you never know, do you?"

"Something even a physician can't predict I guess," said Dr. Ishling.

"Thanks again Doc, we won't keep you any longer."

Twenty-four

"So what have you got for me, Doc?"

"Well, cause of death was an overdose of heroin. There was a puncture wound in his right arm. Funny though, no other tracks—looks like he had never taken it before. There were a few other anomalies."

"Like what?" March asked.

"Like the bruise on the back of his skull."

"Bruise? Like he fell perhaps?"

"No, consistent with a blow to the head by a blunt instrument."

"Some thing like a lamp? Hammer? Chair?"

"Nope, none of those. You'll have to find something that has a shoehorn type shape, like the top part of an egg, say, only flat. No, I'd say it was a pistol, and it occurred shortly before his death."

"That's interesting," March said. "First observation said he died in his sleep."

"Well, he was unconscious before he died. If that's any help."

"Thanks, was there anything else?"

"Judging from the deterioration of the liver, I'd say this guy boozed it up a lot. The liver wasn't exactly the same age as the guy if you know what I mean. He abused it pretty good. In addition, although the lab found hydrogen cyanide in that candle wax, there are no traces of that in his system. That did not contribute to his death."

"We knew he drank pretty heavily. But, his wife insists he never did any hard drugs—marijuana but nothing worse."

"We did find traces of that in his hair follicles, but it didn't kill him. Probably didn't help his lungs any, but didn't kill him."

"Appreciate your input. Can you have that written report on my desk by tomorrow?"

"Sure thing, detective. I've dictated it all and the secretary can type it up right away."

"Forensics called while you were over at the medical examiners office," the receptionist said as March passed her desk.

"Good, I'll call them right back."

"Finger prints on the match book by the candle? Whose? Can you tell? Do me a favor would you run them up against a set of Shorty, ah, Jimmy Delegano's prints just for the record."

The candle residue did show evidence of hydrogen cyanide, so that part of Danielle and JC's story was true. The puncture wound and the bruise tell more. March was glad the medical examiner did not find evidence of any cyanide in the body. He didn't want Danielle to have to face an inquisition. He would find a way to keep that bit of forensic evidence from ever being part of the trial when they found the guy who did do this.

Twenty-five

Detective March pulled up to the wrought iron gate of the Ord estate and pushed the button on the intercom. While he waited, he wondered about their reaction to Danielle's news about their son's death. They had taken care of getting the body transferred from the morgue and they were handling all the funeral arrangements, leaving Danielle without anything but memories of her last view of Randy. A heck of a last look at the man she loved once.

"Yes," a feminine voice said.

"I'm Detective March of the Durango police department. I called earlier. I have an appointment to meet with Mr. and Mrs. Ord," he told the box on the rock gatepost. He heard the gate click and whir as it began to open.

"Come ahead. Someone will meet you at the main door."

The driveway, lined with oaks, was a good quarter of a mile he figured. The lawns looked manicured, flowerbeds interspersed spreads of golf course-like lawns. March couldn't help but drive slowly to take in the view. The mountains jutted against the skyline, almost framing the huge field stone and log house.

"I could park my house, garage and a couple of the neighbors' places in this house," he mused. He parked his car in a space beside the front door and walked the field stone walkway to the steps. A maid opened the door just as he reached for the knocker, an ornate gold eagle perched on a globe.

Gargoyles guarded either side of the entrance. What an odd combination this house was, partly Old World Victorian and partly old West, as though Mr. Ord liked the west and Mrs. Ord preferred merry old England, or was it the other way around? The confused decor of the house made it seem as though someone could not make up his, or her, mind what he or she liked.

The maid led him through a vestibule into a sitting room with a cathedral ceiling. Floor to ceiling bookshelves covered the wall around the massive stone fireplace. Heavy ranch furniture formed a semi-circle in front of the hearth. A tiny woman with snow-white hair sat at a desk in a corner of the room. She turned as March entered.

"Mrs. Ord, Mr. March is here," the maid announced to the woman, who March was sure had seen him and realized who he was by now. They did have an appointment after all.

"Thank you Rose. Would you let Mr. Ord know that Mr. March is here? And do bring some coffee. Would you care for a piece of apple pie with your coffee, Mr. March?" she asked as she came toward him with her hand extended. March took her hand, "No, thank you, coffee would be fine."

"Randolph, this is Mr. March from the Durango Police Department, " she said as a tall silver-haired man entered the room. He extended his hand.

"Please, won't you sit down?" she said as she demurely perched on the edge of an overstuffed wing-back chair. March was reminded of what people meant when they said a woman of breeding. She did seem imposing for all of her small 5'3" frame. Randolph Ord stood behind the chair resting his arm on the back.

"What is it you want from us, Detective?" Mrs. Ord asked after the maid had left the room.

"I have a few questions I need to ask you about Randy. I'm sorry to trouble you during your time of grief but I firmly believe there is more to this case than it seems."

"What do you mean?" Mr. Ord asked, coming around the chair and sitting on the sofa between March and Mrs. Ord's chair.

"I'm not at liberty to discuss that until we put some more pieces together. Do you have any idea what kind of business your son was involved in?"

"No business," Mrs. Ord answered indignantly. "He hasn't done a thing since he finished college except party."

"I understood he was doing some part-time work for a man named James Delegano, driving a truck or something like that," March said.

"He didn't drive a truck. He would have nothing to do with manual labor. He's an Ord," she snarled.

Out of the corner of his eye, March saw Randolph Ord crumple. He seemed to shrivel up as though the words Beatrice Ord spit out crucified him. He walked over to the second couch by the fireplace and sat down.

"Where did he get his money to live on?" March asked looking directly at Mr. Ord.

Mrs. Ord answered for him, while Mr. Ord stared blankly at the floor. "I have no idea, I wasn't about to give him another dime until he changed his ways. His father and I agreed if he couldn't be a part of the family business, he needn't bother trying to get money from us either. Isn't that right, Randolph?"

The words seemed to strike Mr. Ord like an electric shock as he lurched from his seat on the sofa, and in staccato steps went to the fireplace.

"Yes, dear." His answer was as meek as his manner.

March wished he could speak to him alone. He didn't seem to share his wife's views at all.

"Now, if that will be all, Mr. March, we really have so much to do preparing for the funeral and all. I'm really not up to this interview and Randolph, losing his only son and heir, certainly doesn't need to be put through much more either. Our son was a drop-out. He dropped out of the family. He dropped out of community and work, and now he's dropped out of life. I don't think there is much more to tell. Let us do our mourning in peace," she said, rising from her chair and crossing toward the foyer. She pulled the bell cord and the maid who had seen him in reappeared.

"Show Mr. March the way out. I'm sorry we couldn't be of any more help. Good day, Mr. March." She retreated in the opposite direction from the front door. March glanced back over his shoulder to see Mr. Ord, head in his hands, slumped on the sofa again. Somehow he'd have to try to get to talk to him alone. Mrs. Ord seemed to run the household as well as Randolph Ord.

March knew he would only antagonize Beatrice if he tried to continue his questioning now. In March's mind Randolph seemed to know something about his son that Beatrice wasn't privy to. Mrs. Ord was used to verbalizing what she thought. He bet the old man was more like him. "Still waters run deep," the old saw his mother always used waved like a red flag in March's head. He needed to talk to Randolph Ord without the powerhouse Beatrice deflecting hard questions from this sensitive man.

Twenty-six

The police had given Danielle permission to get on with cleaning out the apartment at Mrs. Peoples' insistence. She said she couldn't have the apartment idle. She needed the money. They had gone through the bedroom but had not checked the rest of the apartment; Danielle breathed a sigh of relief at that.

Danielle packed the trash bag with the empty beer cans, old newspapers, magazines, and all the other trash that had been strewn around the rooms. She regretted telling the landlady that she would clean the place. But it was one way to get their security deposit back and she desperately needed the money. Most of Randy's clothes were gone already. His sister Ruth had came and cleaned them and Randy's other belongings out of the apartment two days after Randy's body was discovered. She seemed anxious to retrieve them—some pretence about the family wanting this bad scene behind them. Ah well, that was the Ord family; ignore the bad, cover the indiscretions, and leave the rest behind.

They knew she was pregnant. They would probably try to pull an Ord scheme to get the baby, too. Danielle wasn't sure she wanted to keep the baby anymore. At first, it seemed like a way to get back at Randy to have his child, the heir to at least half of the Ord fortune. She still loved the man she had married despite the mess he had put her through, despite what she had contemplated doing. Despite her leaving, she could not deny she still had feelings for the man.

Danielle slid her hand in the back of the drawer trying to be sure she didn't leave anything in the far reaches of the desk. Her hand brushed against a small box. Underneath it she felt a card. She pulled both items to the front of the drawer.

Tears involuntarily spilled down her cheeks. She opened the box and held up the tiny gold chain with the heart charm, the ankle bracelet Randy had given her that first Valentine's Day what now seemed so long ago. She sat down on the floor, unclasped the chain, and placed it around her ankle. She had forgotten about it. After he had given it to her they had a horrible argument. He had been drinking while he waited for her to come home from work and as usual one wrong word and he went ballistic. He had stormed out and she hadn't seen him again for days. She couldn't even remember what had provoked him. She only remembered she had put the bracelet away and vowed she would never look at it again.

Slowly and pensively, she removed the card from its envelope. It was a thick card with Helen Steiner Rice poetry that spoke of love, friendship and togetherness. He had signed it *I will love you always, Randy*. She held the card close to her heart and rocked back and forth still sitting on the floor. Now he was gone—gone forever. She would never feel his arms around her again. He would never hold their child. Somehow, the terrible events of the last months didn't seem to matter. All she remembered was the love they had shared in the beginning before the drinking. She had no idea why he had started drinking so heavily. Was it the jobs he never got? Was it the fact that she worked and he couldn't seem to find a job? Would she ever know the answer to those questions? She placed the card in the box she had just finished packing and hauled it into the kitchen where the others were.

She took out the vacuum and began vigorously cleaning the kitchen. The drone of the machine drowned the thoughts in her head. She felt the soothing hum as one would feel meditation. The action always did that to her. Whenever she had a problem to sort through it seemed if she got out the vacuum and cleaned the apartment, the answer would materialize from deep with in her. Would there be enough vacuuming in the whole world to fill the void she was feeling now? Tears ran down her face while she pulled and pushed with all the intensity she could summon.

She tore the cushions off the ragged old couch to vacuum under them. There laid a cassette tape. She picked it up and read the label—"The Way Home" scrawled in Randy's handwriting. What? Where had this come from? She put the tape in her shirt pocket. She didn't have time or the means to listen to it at that moment. Mrs. Peoples was supposed to meet her at 3:00 to return the security deposit if the apartment was clean and the same way as when they had rented it.

Danielle vacuumed furiously. She washed windows and dusted down the ragged old shades with an ammonia-soaked cloth. When she had finished, she checked every room to be sure she hadn't missed anything. She desperately needed the money and Mrs. Peoples was sure to try to find some reason not to give it back. She sat down on one of the kitchen chairs and waited for the landlady. The place gave her the creeps now, knowing that Randy had died here made it worse. She decided to wait outside. She could not stand the memories locked in what was once her home.

"Thanks, Mrs. People's," Danielle said as she tucked the check for half the security deposit into her pocket.

"Hrmmph!" Mrs. Peoples said, turned on her heel and went back into the apartment building.

Twenty-seven

Danielle wasn't consciously aware of the train picking up speed as she got closer to the tracks. The shwoop, shwoop of the wheel arm forced her to walk in time to its beat as though she were hypnotized. She loved the Silverton Narrow Gauge. The sound of the whistle triggered some long ago memory, a memory she had never quite figured out. It always made her want to cry or something. She felt like something tied her to the train, something missing, something she should know but didn't. Maybe long ago her life or someone she loved had ended his life in a railroad accident. She kept walking, ignoring the whistle and the rush of her thoughts, like the wheel arms, dashed back and forth, clouding any knowledge that she was still walking toward the tracks.

It would be so easy, so quick. A train, no matter how fast it was traveling would end all this misery she couldn't seem to shake. She felt herself being tugged toward the railcars as if by some unseen force.

Danielle had not noticed Sandy March coming up the street behind her. She didn't see any faces in the wave of people that pushed past her. Trance-like she walked in time to the rhythm, the swoosh, swoosh. She didn't notice anything that cold October morning except the doleful whistle of the Narrow

Gauge as it approached the crossing. It seemed to be calling her, telling her to hurry, to get on board, to leave this place and go where the whistle blew her. She didn't hear the shouts. She didn't hear her name being called. It did not register that the clap, clap, slap noise was of some one running behind her.

Suddenly a hand grasped her shirt and pulled her out of the hypnotic state she was in. She welcomed the broad-shouldered warmth of Sandy March's embrace

"What the hell are you doing?" he shouted at her above the rumble of the passing train.

"I-I don't know," she stammered her body trembling against his chest.

"I didn't mean to yell, but you scared me to death. Were you trying to kill yourself? You're no match for a locomotive, you would have been hamburger if I hadn't grabbed you," he said holding her close not wanting to let her go. Danielle pushed herself back from his embrace. When her deep blue eyes met his, they seemed to be pleading. They were not the eyes of a strong, determined woman she had tried to make outsiders think she was.

"I don't know what came over me. I didn't even see it. All I remember is the whistle," she said. She was still shaking. March offered her his jacket.

"Here, put this on. Let's go get a cup of coffee. We need to warm you up and calm you down. Or is it me, who needs calming down?" he asked, smiling at her.

"I'd like that," she said the faint beginnings of a smile turning up the corners of her petite mouth.

The waitress brought their coffee with some small talk about the nip in the October air, and then she left them to their nervous silence. Sandy was the first one to break the heavy weight of the tension. "Are you okay? I mean, what were you thinking about that almost got you run over by a train anyway?"

Concern knitted his sandy eyebrows into a funny V above his eyes that made Danielle smile.

"I honestly don't know. It's been such an awful day. I had just finished cleaning my old apartment. That crotchety old landlady would only give me back half the security deposit. She said it would be a real hard place to rent now that someone had died there. So, who was going to know that unless she told them? It's just so unfair. I really was counting on that money with the baby coming and all."

March looked at her in surprise. He had not realized she was pregnant.

Danielle saw the surprise on his face. "Oh, you didn't know. Yes, I am pregnant. The baby isn't due until April. JC is the only other person who knows. Well, Randy knew, not that it made any difference in our relationship." She stared down into the coffee cup.

March thought she looked like she was looking for answers in some imagined tea leaves at the bottom of her cup. "Randy is part of the reason I was looking for you this afternoon," March said reaching for her hand. "We finally got the results of the autopsy back. His death was not accidental. At least we don't believe so anymore." He watched Danielle's face darken as he spoke.

"What do you mean?"

"The autopsy showed suffocation associated with an overdose of heroin."

"Randy never touched that stuff. He did a little marijuana, but never the hard stuff—never," she said as a look of total disbelief came across her face.

"We found one puncture wound on his right arm. There's something else that makes us think it wasn't accidental. We also found a bruise on the back of his head. We think someone knocked him out and then shot him up on heroin, hoping to make it look like an overdose."

"Oh, my god! That's awful. Who-who would want to do something like that?" she asked in obvious surprise

"I was hoping you might be able to give me a clue," he said. "We didn't find anything to give us a who, why or anything. I will have to start talking to his friends and acquaintances all over again with a different slant on the questions."

"I can't believe any of his friends would have done something like that. Randy was the party host of all times. They hung on him like bad breath. Besides, they're all a bunch of spineless dropouts."

"What do you know of a guy called Shorty? His real name is Jimmy Delegano."

"That creep? He came around about once a month or so to see Randy. I told Randy I didn't like him and didn't want him in our apartment. Randy said he was harmless and he brought the party goodies. Saved Randy from having to track it down on the street. He thought there was less chance that he would get caught with drugs, seeing as how Shorty delivered them. He just seemed like a mobster to me, you know the TV kind with attitude and muscle following him everywhere."

"I need to ask you one more thing Danielle. You make candles, right?" Sandy hated the question he needed to ask next. He hoped there was some explanation, something that didn't incriminate this lovely young girl. The look of fright that flashed over her face told him what he needed to ask.

"Y-yes, why?" she stammered.

"We found a candle next to the bed that had been burned all the way down. I guess a puddle of wax that must have been a candle would be a better way of putting it. The wax had cyanide traces in it. Do you know anything about that?"

"It was burned? Burned all the way down?" Danielle showed the panic that was enveloping her.

"Take it easy, it didn't kill him. Whoever lit it did so after he was dead. There were no traces that he had inhaled any cyanide. It's just another lead I have to follow up," March said trying to sound reassuring. He could have bitten his tongue off rather than cause the pain he saw in the blue-eyed beauty across from him

"I-I," she stammered. "I did make a candle with cyanide in it. I did plan to light it. I couldn't deal with his abuse anymore. I wanted out and he wouldn't let me go. I didn't know what else to do. But you have to believe me—I didn't light it. I went to the apartment that night to do it. I thought he was asleep. I realize now he must have already been dead. But I couldn't do it. I just couldn't. You believe me, don't you?"

"What I don't understand Danielle is why you didn't just leave. There are places you could go that would provide shelter. You could have a restraining order put on him. Why would you plot to take his life?" March needed some answers to these questions he'd been asking himself ever since he first met Danielle. She was pretty, intelligent and fun to be with—why would she stay with a monster like that Randy?

Danielle, tears threatening to spill from her eyes, shook her head. "I don't know. He threatened that I would never get away from him. He said he could always find me and he'd bring me back home where I belonged. He wasn't the same man I fell in love with, but I still loved him. I prayed he would change. When he didn't, and when Ruth told me about the family and all, I thought if we got married, if he had a family of his own, surely he'd change. He'd go back home to his family and make things right."

"JC told you there was no hope. She told you to get out before something terrible happened. She was your trusted friend and she offered to help you."

"I know, I know. It just—well, it looked so hopeless to try. Then with the baby coming and all, I didn't want him to grow up fatherless. I know it was stupid now. I know what I planned to do was insane. But, I didn't actually go through with it," she said, sobbing.

March handed her a tissue; "Where did you get the cyanide?"

"He had some with his metallurgical kit he had used in school. He said they used to take the stuff to sell for extra cash. He said he never sold his last vile. It was in the closet at the apartment. He would never know I had taken the tiny amount I used. I was just so desperate. You have to understand."

March was pleased that she told him about the backpack and cyanide. It meant that she was not deliberately trying to hide anything.

"I do believe you, Danielle," he said taking her hand in his. "I do believe you. Since it wasn't the murder weapon, you shouldn't have to worry any longer about it. Some one must have lit it though. Did you tell anyone about what you had planned to do?"

"Only JC—oh yes, Thelma. She would come in and sit sometimes while I was working on my candles. Sometimes we'd go have a drink together and rave about our men troubles. I told her. I doubt she'd remember though. She never remembered from one minute to the next what anyone told her. Blonde to the roots as they say," Danielle said.

"I'm afraid all the evidence is pointing directly at you. You had motive, you had means, and you knew his routine."

"I didn't do it. You said he overdosed on heroin. Randy didn't do the hard stuff. He never would. He drank, he did a joint once in a while, but no, he would never do the hard stuff. Besides, he couldn't afford it, not on what I made. We barely could keep the apartment and food on the table. I brought the night's leftovers home from The Office Bar a couple times a week or we would really be hurting. "

March wanted to believe Danielle. He had to believe her. He wanted her to be a part of his life. He wanted to take care of her and show her how real love should be.

"Okay, Danielle. I guess that's all for now. But you stay close okay? And, young lady, keep your distance from those trains. Nothing is so bad that it can't be fixed. If you need help, you come to me, promise?" March asked.

"Sure, I've got nowhere to go anyway."

"Good, now do you need a ride home, or could I walk with you back to JC's?"

"No, Mr. March,"

"Sandy, please."

"Okay, Sandy," she said a smile starting and then flitting away as quickly as it came. "JC is meeting me and we're going shopping before work today. Thanks anyway."

"Danielle, I know this is probably out of line but, do you have a way to get to Randy's funeral? Assuming you want to go that is." March said hoping the answer was no she did not have a way, but yes she wanted to be there.

"I thought maybe I'd try to get a bus," Danielle said.

"I'd like to go," March said holding her gaze with his. "I mean, you know they usually say whoever was responsible for a death sometimes shows up at the funeral and besides it would give me a chance to see people with their guards down. I'd be happy to take you. If you want to go."

Danielle did not answer right away she seemed to be processing the question and weighing it in her mind.

"No strings attached," he added quickly hoping to convince her that she could go with him.

"Thanks," she said lowering her eyes. "I don't know how well that would set with Randy's parents though."

"Don't they know the two of you had split up already?"

"I don't know what they know for sure."

"Well, it really shouldn't matter what other people think anyway, Danielle. I am just a friend. To me it would be perfectly logical that a friend brings you to your husband's funeral for support. We could ask JC to go along if that would make you feel better."

"I'm sure she couldn't. She has two jobs and school. I don't know where she would find the time. Let me think about it Mr. Ma— I mean Sandy," she said with a forced smile. "I'll call you and let you know tomorrow, okay?"

"Sure, but promise you'll give it some serious thought. I am planning on going anyway. It would save you some money and give me some company on that long drive."

"I'll call you," she said.

March left the restaurant with a million thoughts swirling in his head. He did mean the part about the killer showing up somewhere in the victim's life afterwards and he felt the funeral might be just the place to really get a handle on Randy's friends, relatives and perhaps the murderer. The job would definitely be more interesting and palatable if Danielle were to accompany him.

~ * ~

Danielle stared out the window after Sandy March. He was really a sweet guy. He did seem to care about people. What would it hurt if she went to Colorado Springs to the funeral with him? She certainly didn't want to face Randy's parents alone. She thought about the trip she tried to make to see them before.

It was after Danielle had made up her mind to get Randy to marry her. Her child would have access to the Ord fortune even if Randy wanted no part of it. Why hadn't he told her about his parents? Why had it taken his sister to tell her? He was the biggest jerk. Well, that part was behind them now. He had married her. She toyed with the small gold band on her finger. Not the wedding she had always dreamed of—no cathedral, no flowing train on a long, white wedding gown, no father to give her away. Ah, but she got a future for her child that would outmeasure any dream she could ever have dreamed for her own future.

Danielle decided that a bus trip seemed natural and logical. She should meet her new in-laws. They should know they were about to become grandparents. She pondered whether the senior Ords would accept her. She debated with herself over and over. For once in her life, she needed to act. She needed to see Randy's family to see their reaction to her. I miss family. I miss my mother. Would the Ords treat me like a daughter? At last, she decided she would never know unless she took the chance and went to them.

She boarded the bus to Colorado Springs with renewed hope. The trip was long, the bus stopping at little out-of-the-way burgs to pick up more passengers. Thoughts and doubts started to plague Danielle. What if they rejected her? What if they had decided to disown their son after all? Why didn't she just have an abortion and forget the whole thing? Get rid of Randy like she planned without checking in with the family?

No, she would never have an abortion, no matter what. If she had to raise her child alone she would, she would love him like she had never been loved. Randy may be a jerk but he had at least given her something to treasure.

By the time she reached Colorado Springs, the doubts and fears had clobbered her self-esteem. She no longer felt confident or capable of standing up to the Ords or anyone. No, she would just return to Durango and let fate run its course. Danielle got off the bus, and went right to the ticket widow to see when the return bus would leave. She didn't have long to wait and she was glad because she was afraid she might change her mind again if she had to wait too long. She would not go to the Ord home. If Randy didn't want her to know about them, that was how it would be, at least, that was, until the baby was born. She went into the small bus stop café to wait the hour until her return trip. She plotted the making of the candle that would rid her of Randy once and for all. These thoughts caused an involuntary shudder to ripple across her and raise goose bumps on her arms.

She sipped her coffee and drew boxes on the napkins. Squared boxes, three-dimensional boxes, shaded boxes, graduated-size boxes. She drew boxes until they called the bus for Durango was ready to depart. Danielle looked at her artwork. She used to doodle in curves, loops, and fanciful lace—open, weaving, hopeful. Now, her doodling was all boxed in, like she felt trapped in the boxes made by other people. She wondered what a psychiatrist would make of her doodling. Actually, she knew exactly what a shrink would say. She didn't need an expert opinion to tell her that her life was off track. Danielle paid for her coffee and boarded the bus back home. That already seemed eons ago. Her life had taken so many abrupt turns in the last week, she was sure she must be chasing her own tail by now.

Danielle felt the cassette tape in her pocket that she had just picked up at the apartment. She needed to listen to it to find out what it meant. She probably should have given it to Sandy March. Maybe it held clues to Randy's murderer. No, she would listen to it first. That was what Randy had wanted. She was sure of that. Maybe she would give it to March on the way to the funeral.

"I guess I've already decided I will be going with him," she said as she made her way out of the restaurant and down the street to meet JC.

Twenty-eight

When Ruth entered her father's hospital room, the machines that were attached to him the day before were silent; he was sitting up and talking with her mother. They both looked up when she entered.

"Hi Dad, how you feeling?" she asked, forcing a smile and holding out both hands to him.

"I'd be a lot better if Randy was alive," he said coarsely.

"I'm sorry Dad. There isn't anything you could have done. It just had to happen with the life style he was leading."

"Ruth, that'll be enough," her mother said sharply.

Ruth kissed her father on the cheek and her look shot daggers at her mother. *Always defending the little son of a bitch, always the dear boy to mommy. I am so sick of it*, she thought trying to hide her true feelings from her father.

"Your father will be out of the hospital tomorrow, I've arranged the funeral for Thursday. We need to get this behind us and start fresh."

"Mother, I've checked out your precious son's so-called wife. She is nothing but a gold digger. She has no family, except an aunt in Wisconsin. She isn't even from around here. You can't be planning to do anything about her bastard child, can you? You don't even know if its Randy's child or not. How could you possibly—"

Beatrice Ord cut Ruth's tirade in two. The look in her eyes told Ruth she had over-stepped her bounds with her mother. "Get out, get out of this room. There is no point in your spreading such lies. Randy was to take over our company. His heir is next in line for that honor and I will do everything I can to see to it that Danielle is part of the Ord family. I plan to offer to provide for her and the child. They can come live with us. Randy would have wanted that."

Ruth looked at the pained expression on her father's face and decided she would not confront her mother on this issue, now. She would handle it her way. She turned abruptly and kissed her father on the cheek. "Gotta go Daddy, I'll talk to you later." She ignored her mother completely and walked out of the room without turning back

Oh, she would handle Danielle all right. All that little bitch wanted was a free meal ticket. I wonder how much she'd take to have an abortion and move back to Wisconsin where she belongs. *Move into the Ord mansion? I hardly think so. Over my dead body.*

Ruth's phone was ringing when she unlocked the door. She looked at her watch. Who would be calling at this hour? She raced to the telephone and answered it.

"Hi. Ruth?"

"Yes, this is Ruth Ord. How may I help you?"

"Ruth, this is Danielle, Randy's wife."

"Oh, you. What do you want?"

"I found something while I was cleaning our apartment, getting ready to move out."

"So, what do I care? We have nothing to talk about anymore."

"Ruth, Randy...he," Danielle paused she wasn't sure just how to tell Ruth what she found and Ruth didn't sound like she wanted anything to do with her or Randy's memory.

"What? I'm awfully busy. I don't have time for games," Ruth said.

"It's important Ruth or I wouldn't bother you. Randy made a tape of something he was involved in. He told me, on the tape, to call you instead of the police, but, he said you would know what to do with it if anything happened to him. I'm scared Ruth. Randy was mixed up in some bad stuff. I don't know why he wanted me to call you, but I don't know what else to do with it. Maybe I should just give it to the police. But I'm trying to follow his instructions. He seemed to think you were the one to call." Danielle could not stop herself once she got started.

"Hold on, hold on. Not so fast. Randy did what?" Ruth cut in.

"He made this tape, a cassette. I found it when I was cleaning the apartment. He titled it "The Ticket Home." I don't know what it means, Ruth, but there's some stuff on it—names, places, things I think you should hear," she said trying to compose herself. "It involves a man the police were asking about, a Shorty, ah, Jimmy Delegano."

"Okay, okay. I'll come down. I have some things I need to do in the morning. I'll hit the road as soon as I can. Will you be home?"

"I have to go to work. Um, I work until closing. I should be done by 2:30. Why don't you meet me at the Country Kitchen about 3?"

"Three in the morning? How about if I just come by the café and you give me the tape? I'll listen to it and let you know what I think we should do."

Danielle didn't know what to do. For some reason, she didn't want to just give up the tape without knowing what Ruth would do with it. She really did not trust Ruth Ord after the last conversation with her knowing how she felt about her brother, Randy.

"I'd rather we listened to it together," she said

"I don't have time for this," Ruth said. "Either you give me the tape, or you can just mail it to me. I won't make a trip for nothing."

Danielle could hear the anger in her voice. Ruth thought of Danielle as another thorn in her side. Randy was the first and of course, she would be, being Randy's wife and all.

"Okay, Ruth. If you promise me you won't leave until we discuss it," Danielle said clutching at straws.

"Yeah, alright" Ruth abruptly hung up the telephone.

Danielle stared at the handset then replaced it in the cradle and fingered the tape. She wondered if perhaps she shouldn't give it to Sandy March anyway. She decided she would wait and talk to Ruth first. Perhaps she could come up with a way to use the information, or get it to the police without jeopardizing the Ord family or her safety. She would wait for Ruth. What was one more day in this bizarre life she was leading? She wasn't at all sure if Ruth would show up.

Again, she thought about calling Sandy and explaining to him what she had found. That wouldn't be what Randy wanted, but what did she care what Randy wanted? He hadn't confided in her about any of this. He hadn't been a real husband to her. Not the way she had wanted and hoped he'd be. So, what if his precious family got into trouble over the mess he was involved in?

She sat down on the couch, not sure what she would do next. She wondered about Mr. Ord, Randy's father. She felt sorry for him living under the thumb of Mrs. Ord, and having a daughter like Ruth. She really didn't want to hurt the family. Maybe she should tell JC what she had found. Maybe JC would tell her or at least help her decide what she should do.

She glanced up at the clock. Too late. JC had already gone to work at Colorado Land Title, her day job. She would have to wait until she saw her tonight at The Office Bar.

Danielle thought she had better make a copy of the tape. She put it into the stereo with a blank cassette on the other side. She turned it on and listened again as she copied it. It was so strange listening to Randy's voice knowing he was dead. "Deliver: Oxycodone hydrochloride—Oxycontin on the street: 6 cases to Paoli, CO. The warehouse on Main St., the west entrance to Amy Stevens. She will sign for it.

Deliver 12 cases to...

Lists and lists—drops and names of people and places. Danielle figured that black market Oxycontin tablets must be big money as Randy quoted payments he would receive at each drop.

Clack! The sound of the tape turning itself off jarred Danielle back to the present. She removed both tapes and put one in the drawer with the rest of her tapes. Nervously Danielle took the other tape, put it in her cosmetic bag, and tucked it into the hobo bag purse she carried. She would not let the tape out of her possession until she was sure what the right move would be.

~ * ~

Danielle turned off the shower and reached for her bath towel. In the kitchen, she rinsed a cup under the faucet and poured herself a cup of coffee. Taking a long sip, she took the coffee with her to the bedroom to dress for work. A cropped white T-shirt from the laundry basket, along with a red tank top. She dug through a pile of clothes on the floor, rejected a pair of stained Levi's and pulled another pair from the heap, dressing quickly. These would have to do. As she squirmed into the Levi's and laid across the bed to zip them because her pregnant belly was in the way.

"Damn." Her waistline was starting to thicken and her tummy barely fit in her jeans. Fine mess she'd gotten herself into this time. She sure couldn't waitress through all this, not at the Office. That place was strictly sexy young female waitresses who weren't afraid to wear the uniforms allowed there. Danielle wondered how long the Dallas cheerleader style uniform would support her expanding body. The only good thing was her breasts were also enlarging. She did not have to stuff and uplift to give her cleavage now.

Danielle did not have time to talk to JC about the tape. Ruth Ord was waiting for her when she got to the Office Bar & Grill. She was glad she decided to make a copy of the tape before she left home.

"Give me the damn tape," Ruth snapped when she spotted Danielle.

Danielle stared at the older woman, wondering why she was so angry. "I thought you would want to help Randy," she said hesitantly

"Look, I do Danielle. It's been a long day and a long drive and I am just tired. Please forgive me I didn't mean to snap."

"Okay, it's in my purse. Just a minute." Danielle said. She watched Ruth nervously checking cars coming down the street and people milling around the bar & grill. She seemed very nervous.

"Here," she said and handed the tape to Ruth. Ruth grabbed the tape and abruptly headed down the street.

"Wait," Danielle called. "When should we meet to discuss the contents?"

"I'll call you," Ruth yelled over her shoulder.

Danielle shrugged. She was glad she had made the copy. It was almost as if Ruth Ord didn't want to be seen with her. Well, she would just have to wait until she heard from her there was nothing more she could do.

Twenty-nine

Ruth listened to the cassette tape Danielle had given her as she was leaving Durango to go back to Colorado Springs. She stopped at a pay phone and called Shorty Delegano.

"I have to talk to you. You've got a real problem. I got a tape from Danielle that implicates you and your boss in some pretty heavy stuff. She was going to give it to the cops but I talked her into letting me do that," Ruth said.

"Wait a minute. Hold on. What are you talking about?" Shorty barked.

"You idiot. How come you weren't more careful when you took care of Randy? He evidently had a tape lying around that outlines the whole scam you and PaPa Belongi had going with the drugs and other crap. Danielle was cleaning the apartment afterwards and she found this tape labeled 'A Ticket Home.' You stupid clown, now we have her to worry about. Can't you do anything right?" Ruth growled into the telephone.

"Don't get your girdle in a twist. We'll take care of her."

"No, no. I don't think so this time. You leave little Danielle to me. It has to look like an accident and you don't seem to be able to handle accidents very well."

"Okay, so you take care of your own messes. I would like that tape however."

"My messes? My messes? If you hadn't botched the job with Randy, none of this would be necessary. You will get the tape when I say you get the tape. I just want you to know there is some very damaging evidence out here and if I ever need it, I will use it." Ruth slammed down the phone.

Maybe she should make a copy of the tape as her insurance against future reprisals by Shorty. Put it in a safe place. He wouldn't dare try to get it or to harm her, would he? She wished she had never decided to take matters into her own hands. If she had left well enough alone Randy would have killed himself with the booze. The problem was she couldn't afford to wait for Randy to commit suicide with the alcohol. With Randy married, it wouldn't be long before the folks discovered the little bitch, and she'd probably have a kid in the works by that time. That little witch had probably only married Randy to get her fingers on his money in the first place.

She began to form a plan to get to Sandy March and tell him all she could to implicate Danielle in the murder of her brother. She'd tell March she didn't come forward earlier because she didn't want to believe that Danielle was capable of murder. If she didn't get Danielle, the murder rap would. She would see to that. She tucked the tape under some folders in her brief case and dialed Sandy March's office on her cell phone.

Ruth decided she would stop in and see Sandy March. She would see what she could do to convince him that Danielle had the perfect motive and opportunity to kill Randy.

Thirty

"Come in Ms. Ord. I've been waiting to talk to you," March said as the woman appeared in the doorway of his office.

"I got your message days ago, but this is the first opportunity I've had. I've been so busy with the company. Dad is in no shape to attend to much since Randy's death. I must admit it hit our family hard although he hasn't really been a part of it for years. What is it you needed to see me about?" she asked as she flung her long blonde hair back away from her too narrow face. The hairdo tended to emphasize her long thin nose and sharp angular features.

"Well, since we know that Randy's death was a homicide, I just wondered if you had any idea who would have wanted to see him dead. It seems you two were still in touch, at least according to Danielle."

"That little harlot. She roped and tied Randy after she found out how much he was worth."

"What do you mean?" March asked, sensing Ruth had no good use for Danielle, but he wondered why.

"It wasn't until my visit that she decided she should marry Randy. He had been beating her around for a while already and she said she was about to leave him. Then, all of a sudden they get married. I thought it was strange at the time. However, she tends to inherit Randy's share of the estate if anything happens to my parents. Therefore, now it all makes perfect sense to me. She's just an opportunist, out to make a quick buck. "

"She seems like a nice person. She hardly seems the kind that would marry for money."

"Looks can be deceiving. She is a calculating, manipulating, hanger-on. As I see it she is the only one who would profit by Randy's death."

"You inherit the Ord fortune if your parents die, don't you? Especially with Randy gone, I'm sure Danielle would not get Randy's full share."

"She will if she's pregnant. My parents have been waiting for a namesake, and they would give their eye teeth to have had an opportunity to realize that dream with Randy as the proud daddy."

"Is she pregnant?" March asked wondering if she knew that her fears were already true.

"Who knows? Likely as not she won't come fortune-hunting until you wrap this thing up so she doesn't appear to have a motive to want Randy knocked off," Ruth said in a bitter tone.

"You said you came to see Randy and that's when you found out about Danielle, is that correct?"

"That's right. Randy had come to me for money to go into a rehabilitation program because he said he had a job opportunity and needed to get straight."

"Did you give him the money?"

"Well, no I didn't. The last time I did, he blew the money and never did get dried out. I had thought about it and thought if he were serious, I'd take him to a treatment center and pay in advance. That way I was sure he would at least get in. Except, when I got to his place, Danielle said that they had had a fight and Randy had taken off. She didn't know when to expect him back if ever."

"What else did you and Danielle talk about?"

"She never knew he had a family. I told her where we were and that since Randy dropped out of college, we hadn't seen him. She was surprised about the college thing too. Obviously she never knew or cared to know anything about Randy or she would have asked him."

"Is it possible that Randy just preferred not to talk about his past, or his family?"

"That doesn't make any sense. He's worth big bucks. We've pulled him out of more scrapes than anyone can imagine. He loved his family. He was just being belligerent because mother wanted him to go into corporate law. He didn't want to work that hard. They spoiled him rotten and then wondered how he got the way he was," she said.

"What do you mean, 'the way he was'?"

"Well, you know, the drinking, drugs and living the way he did with all the scum hanging around and that Danielle, cheap little cocktail waitress. I mean, really, my parents were thoroughly disgusted about it all."

"Were they disgusted enough to write him out of their wills?"

"They would never be that disgusted, not with their darling little boy. That would never happen in this lifetime," she said with vengeance in her voice.

"Someone said Randy was working for some trucking outfit up near Denver, doing occasional jobs. Do you happen to know anything about that?"

"Randy? I doubt it. He hated work. If someone said he was working, they were lying. Besides, every time he applied for any job, my parents would find out while the prospective employers were doing background checks and they'd send one of their hired idiots to find him and drag him home. Randy would go ballistic and swear he'd never work again if they didn't leave him alone to run or ruin his own life the way he saw fit. So to answer your question, I sincerely doubt it."

"So, as far as you know he wasn't working anywhere. Is that right?"

"That's it," she said.

"And you can't think of anyone who would want to see Randy dead, other than Danielle, as far as you're concerned?"

"You got it. Now if there is nothing further I do have a company to run." She stood and started for the door.

March noticed how masculine she appeared. Even her suit had a manish cut to it. She wore work oxfords instead of heels. "Thank you for coming in, Ms. Ord. If you think of anything else, please give me a call." He opened the door for her.

March wondered about her attitude toward Danielle. It seemed to him born out of jealousy, or vengeance. The Danielle he had come to know would never be guilty of such a heinous thing as killing her husband, even if she had made the cyanide-laced candle. She couldn't light it. She told him that and he believed her. He was a good judge of character. If any one was suspicious and had a motive, it was Ruth Ord. She didn't appear too happy with her family's treatment, being overlooked because of the shadow of brother Randy. Maybe he needed to find some people who knew Ruth and see if he could get a feel for who she was exactly.

Danielle's smile warmed Sandy March somewhere near the pit of his stomach. Her eyes caught him off guard—deep expressive eyes that had a depth beyond the physical plane. He had felt an instant attraction to her. When he interviewed her that first time he watched for any reaction that might give him a clue that she knew anything about Randy's death. He thought about the brown hair that hung almost to her waist and her sad eyes that were sad even before the news of her husband's death. March felt an urge to put his arms around her and shelter her from the world. She was such an innocent-looking waif, but it was more than that. He felt drawn to her by something deep inside himself. He suddenly felt sorry for the young woman twisted by the painful news he delivered. Her eyes had reminded him then of the deer-in-the-headlights-of-an-oncoming-car look he'd seen before. His hand automatically ran across the scar over his eyebrow, the reminder of the deer crashing through his windshield.

The evidence against Danielle as the murderer of Randy Ord was continuing to mount. This bothered March. Yet, he had to consider all the possibilities. There was Danielle's candle-making hobby, the residue left on the nightstand by a candle with traces of cyanide in the wax, especially in light of Thelma's testimony that Danielle had told her of a plan to kill Randy with a cyanide-laced candle. It could have been a moment of anger that led her to devise this plan or it could have been she planned to carry out the threat. March doubted the latter. Now Ruth had come forward with what she knew.

First the elder Ords didn't know about her and supposedly Danielle didn't know they existed, but she had because Ruth told her. Then she and Randy married after her visit from Ruth. That would, in a court of law, probably serve as evidence that she planned to get to the Ord fortune. It certainly didn't convince March, but a jury would find it suspicious.

There was a problem with Ruth's theory. What about the heroin that actually killed Randy? She said he did drugs. Danielle said he never went farther than marijuana and it appeared from all his acquaintances that was all he ever tried.

So, where did the heroin come from? Why would Danielle want to kill him? She could probably get plenty of support money if she was pregnant. Was he letting his feelings get in the way of his job? He wasn't sure he could answer that question because he didn't know.

He had fallen in love with Danielle. There was no doubt about that. What if she did turn up guilty? Maybe he should get himself taken off the case. No, he couldn't do that. He wouldn't know what they uncovered until it was too late. No, he had to stay on the case for Danielle's sake.

March took out the sticks Cherokee Joe had given him so long ago and laid them in a pile on the desk. He started the solitaire game Joe had taught him. First he laid out the red stick as the homicide victim, and then he laid the plain sticks out to represent people who stood to gain from his death. Ruth and Danielle were prime suspects in this category. Something was missing he could feel it. He just didn't know what. Somewhere Shorty Delegano played a part.

He pulled the file with Shorty Delegano's rap sheet in it from under the others. Extortion, muscle, a known fence, he had been picked up on several charges of carrying a controlled substance. None of the raps showed he was convicted of anything. Not even so much as a traffic ticket clouded his record with a conviction. What was his tie to Randy Ord? More than his friends were telling him he was sure of that. He would talk to the weakest link in the circle of Randy's friends. There must be a suspicion, if not knowledge, of what his involvement was with Delegano. March called Lesh in and asked him to help him figure out which of Randy's friends was most likely to know about Randy's dealings with Shorty Delegano.

They ruled out Danielle immediately because all his friends seem to agree that she never had much to do with Randy's party life.

"What we need to do is talk to one of them that doesn't have much backbone and wouldn't want to wind up in a cell with no chance to get a fix or drink for a couple days," Lesh said flipping through the pages of notes he had on the interviews with Randy's friends.

"I don't know why I didn't think of this before. Check out all their names and see if any of them have a rap sheet. If we come up with one, he maybe our weak link."

"I'll get right on it," Lesh said.

Thirty-one

The basset hound raised his head just enough to peer at the truck coming down main street. March recognized Cherokee Joe's constant companion, "Spirit of Fog." The black and white basset hound took life like Joe did, leisurely. They were a perfect pair. March knew Joe must be in the Feed Store, his favorite hangout.

"Hey, Sandy," Roger Melford said as he entered the front door. "Long time no see. Aren't you a little out of your territory?"

"Sort of, Mr. Melford. I was looking for old Cherokee. Figured I'd find him here if he wasn't home."

"Come on in, set a spell. Roger and me was just hashing out the finer points of ranching in these parts. Want some coffee?" Cherokee offered, sliding down a bit on the bench to make room for March.

"Sure, why not?" March accepted the tin cup and sitting down next to Cherokee Joe.

Cherokee was actually a Southern Ute. But he always said, "To the white man, the only Indians they knew existed were Apache and Cherokee." So everyone called him Cherokee Joe and he let them rather than argue about it. "After all," he asked,

"What's in a name? I know who I am and that's all that counts."

"What brings you all the way over here?" Joe asked.

"Got a real puzzler of a case and thought I could pick your brain for a while and see what you think," March replied.

"You must mean that Ord feller. Saw that in the papers. A shame, such a young man. His family must be devastated," Joe said. "Finish your coffee and we'll head out home. You can tell me all about it over a good home-cooked meal."

March watched as the old man stacked the wood in the fire pit. He remembered back as a boy when they first moved to Colorado, how he had seen Cherokee Joe lighting the river on fire. He thought the old Indian was magic or something. Those eons ago when his imagination ruled, before he dealt with the impossibilities of human black magic on a regular basis, he thought Joe was old then, but he never changed. Sometimes March thought he must have been born looking exactly the way he looked now.

Cherokee Joe seemed by far the sanest and un-magical of all the weird people he had met in his line of work. Joe seemed to have a razor-sharp perception of things that had helped March solve many a case in the past. So, when he was really stymied he would come to Joe to get some help in sorting out exactly what it was he had but couldn't see. Just as Joe explained the fire on the river as being the natural gas deposits from the wealth below the earth's crust in these parts, Joe always seemed to find the logical explanation, the one clue March kept missing in his most troubling cases.

"So tell me Sandy, what's got you so all-fired bamboozled about this case?" Joe sat down beside March on the old wool blanket.

"Well..." March began.

March watched Joe as he stared at the fire. He watched as he studied the skies as though he had never seen them before. The old man looked ancient sitting in the glow of the firelight. March knew he was at least 80, but how many years beyond that couldn't be detected by tracing the lines meandering from forehead to chin and back again. He had seen much and knew more than anyone March knew. He always had a knack for worrying a problem to a reasonable conclusion. March knew he depended on him for help more than he probably should. What would happen when Joe was gone? He would have to rely on himself or technology, which to March did not sound like a reasonable substitute for the Shaman Cherokee Joe.

"Well, my boy, what is it that has you picking at fleas today?" He asked in his warm, thick voice.

"It's this murder case. But for the sharp eye of our head of forensics, we would have thought this guy died in his sleep, although he was obviously in too good a shape to die suddenly, for no apparent reason. The suspects we've come up with so far don't fit the murderer profile I see in my mind. It looks to me like a…well, I just don't know at this point."

"Why don't we start at the beginning? You tell me who, what, when, where and your guess at why and we'll work through it. Maybe you will be able to see something hiding in the bushes that you haven't rattled clear yet," Joe said.

As March explained the case to Joe, he laid out little sticks on the ground in a pattern of victim, suspects, and acquaintances. They formed a sort of fan. March noticed there was a hole in the fan big enough for two more sticks. "It looks like I don't have a full house in the suspect area of your fan, Joe."

"You're right. Now who are you overlooking? Who would gain from the death of a millionaire's son?"

March began to list the people. "Danielle, his widow, and their child. Although she made the cyanide candle, it didn't cause his death so it doesn't matter if she had lit it. There's Ruth, his sister, who stood to lose control of the family fortune if Danielle and child were accepted into the picture. Shorty, he wasn't yet a suspect, didn't seem to have a connection, and what would he gain and yet his name keeps popping up in all the investigations. I can't think of another person, and Shorty doesn't fit, he doesn't have a motive, yet his fingerprints were on the matchbook cover found by the bed. Problem is that there were two other sets of prints that we can't match up with anything we have on record," March said.

"Who could give him a motive? I think someone gave him a motive. I think he slithers on his belly through this whole mess. It's up to you to find his connection to the Ord fortune," Joe said waving across the pattern the sticks had made in the sand.

"What bothers me most is that the whole thing seems to point at Danielle, and yet she is the most innocent, trusting young thing you could ever hope to meet. I sure don't want it to be her," March said.

"I could tell you had strong feelings for the woman. Perhaps you could bring her out to see me. Maybe my heart won't be in the way of the facts and I can talk to her. Get a feel for who she is, and her connections here. She did make up that cyanide candle in the first place. So she isn't as innocent as you'd like me to believe."

"You're probably right. I know my feelings have a tendency to get in the way. But, goll darn it, I just can't believe she'd do something like that. I'll see if I can get her to ride over here and see you in the next day or two," March said feeling a little like a schoolboy bringing a date home for approval. "Right now I better get back. I've got a lot of work to do. I appreciate all your help, Joe."

The ride home was more time than March wanted to think about this case. His mind kept seeing Danielle injecting heroin into the arm of the father of her child. She hated him now with good reason. However, he didn't think she was capable of killing him no matter what, and where would she get the heroin?

In his deep dark thoughts he almost hit a deer crossing the road. He swerved to avoid the collision and wound up down an embankment. Dazed but unharmed he put the jeep in four-wheel drive and tried to back out of the ditch. The tires spun angrily, but inch-by-inch he climbed back onto the road. *I better get a handle on this case before I kill myself trying.* He slowly wound his way around the mountain path that had become a narrow road to civilization over the last decade.

Thirty-two

I may as well call the little bitch before I get out of Durango.

Ruth dialed The Office Bar & Grill number. "Danielle Ord please," she said to the male voice that answered. In a few minutes, a female voice said, "This is Danielle."

"This is Ruth Ord. I wanted to let you know I listened to the tape. It's probably a figment of Randy's overactive imagination. He always was a little paranoid. He always wove tales around perceived instances."

"I really don't think this is just make-believe Ruth. Where would he get all those names? And he talks about warehouses and stuff. I didn't know he drove a truck. I knew he was gone for long stretches of time but it was usually after one of our fights. He always took off after we argued. Maybe he was driving the truck then," Danielle said.

"I don't really believe it, Danielle. I have so much to deal with right now with the funeral and everything so I will have to put this on hold. However, I will get a private eye I know to check it out on the sly and see what he can turn up. Meantime I don't think it would be wise to tell anyone about the tape. You know, just wait until I have time to verify it. We wouldn't want to start some dirty mess that has nowhere to go."

"Okay, I guess you could be right." Danielle paused, then asked, "Why would he make the tape though? It seems he was concerned that something might happen to him. Why, Ruth?"

"I don't have an answer for you. Look, I'll check it out and get back to you as soon as I can. You don't have to worry about it, but keep your mouth shut."

Ruth was not sure Danielle would keep her mouth shut. She was such a persistent little gnat. *I have to think of some way to shut her up permanently before she spills the beans to that Sandy March.*

Now there is a real piece of work, Danielle thought. *Detective, my ass.* He isn't even dry behind the ears yet. He'll never figure this one out and with what I told him Danielle is his prime suspect right now.

She slammed the Porsche into gear and screeched away from the curb leaving Durango and Danielle and all the damn "D" problems behind.

Thirty-three

St Joseph's Catholic Church was filled when Sandy March and Danielle Ord arrived. The greeters directed them to the Ord family side. Danielle stopped at a pew toward the rear of the church. March followed her in. She looked stunning in her simple black dress and veiled hat. Almost no one wore hats any more but it added a touch to Danielle that March appreciated. She hadn't spoken much since they arrived in Colorado Springs. It was like she had been transported to a world devoid of, or at least incapable of, speech. At the funeral home, she had been silent and withdrawn, and since then, she had been locked inside her cocoon. No matter what he did, he could not seem to break her free.

The service was long and drawn out. March listened as the priest spouted the legacy of the philanthropic Ords—blood of the community and the world, how the son, Randolph Ord III was swiped away before his good could reach the world. Yea, and what he did to Danielle and the life he lived was far from the saint Randy Ord, according to the priest. *Blasphemy.* He swallowed the word before it could escape his lips. Altar boy, outstanding student—the list went on *ad nausea.*

March fidgeted like he was a child, sitting between his parents for a hundred Sunday mornings as a child. March thought how torturous this was for the family surrounded by grief, trapped in a world that could not console them. Perhaps he was wrong. He always hated funerals and maybe he was just juxtaposing his feelings on others. Maybe the church offered them the only consolation there was in a death that ripped someone away before their lives had come full circle. He studied the backs of mourners' heads. Some bowed, some sniffling back sorrow, a cough, a child's restless squeaks and parental shushing...He felt Danielle heave a sigh and dab at silent tears. How could she still love the jerk after what he had done?

At the cemetery, March had an opportunity to observe the mourners. Two men in uniforms stood on the periphery of the family group. He had seen the tractor rig at the church, E-Line Trucking. He made a mental note to check it out. The brief graveside service ended and Beatrice Ord made her way to Danielle's side.

"Dear, we're having immediate family over to the house for a meal if you and Mr. March would care to join us, I'd like to talk to you about a letter I received from Randy shortly before he-he...died," she said holding on to Danielle's elbow.

"We have a long drive ahead back to Durango." She hesitated glancing up at March.

"It doesn't matter to me, Danielle. We can take some time. We really aren't in a hurry."

"Please, dear, it would mean so much to Randolph. We never got a chance to get to know you before this tragedy. You are a part of the family, you know," she pleaded.

"Okay, sure. We'll stop by," Danielle said.

Beatrice Ord carried herself with the stature that money seems to give to spine. March could not put an age to her, but knowing both Randy's age and Ruth's, she had to be well into her seventies he thought.

March looked for the truckers. They were already in the tractor and leaving the cemetery. He escorted Danielle back to his car and they headed for the Ord Mansion.

"That E-line truck over there—did you happen to see the two men at the cemetery? They were kind of standing way back from the family," March asked Danielle as he pulled the car away from the curb.

"Oh, yeah. I recognized one of them. I have no clue who the other is."

"Who is the one you recognize?"

"Horn. He was one of the regulars at Randy's parties. His girlfriend, Thelma, was really nice. She's the one I told about the candle, remember?"

"I do remember. Horn is the one we never found at home to interview. Does Thelma go with him when he's on the road?"

"Not all the time. Pretty much though. She said she loves a chance to see the country. She never minded living out of a suitcase. I'm not sure I could handle that."

Danielle stared out the window. March thought she was in a different world again. He didn't quite know what to make of this very introverted person.

"Pretty impressive service," he said trying to make conversation.

"Yeah. I wonder what Mrs. Ord really wants?"

"Why does she have to want something, Danielle? You are a part of the family. Widowed before you got a chance to really be part of them, but part of them you are."

"After meeting Ruth, I don't trust any of them. Why was Randy so secretive about them? Why didn't Ruth help him out? Why didn't she tell his parents about us? She knew long before Randy was…well, she knew. I don't understand."

She was on the verge of tears again. March could not stand to see her cry.

"Hey, take it easy. The only way to find out the answers to your questions is to go there and hear what she has to say. Maybe she really just wants to welcome you to the family. Maybe she wants to see if she can help you out financially or anything. Wait and see. Don't expect the worst. I'll be right there. We can always get in the car and boogie if you don't like the song you're hearing. Okay?"

Danielle blew her nose and nodded her head. She dried the tears that had started to trickle down her pale face.

"Chin up, girl. We're here," he said with a sigh. He wasn't anxious to do this himself although he did want to see these people in a more relaxed setting. Mrs. Ord hadn't let on that she remembered him from the interview he had had with her earlier. March was sure she remembered though. That woman had a mind like a black widow spider's web. There was very little that would escape her memory. He was absolutely sure of that.

Beatrice Ord took Danielle under her wing almost immediately when they arrived. She left March to fend for himself, which he was glad to do. He could snoop and listen in on conversations without being noticed. Mrs. Ord buzzed the widowed, younger Mrs. Ord around the room introducing her to a myriad of relatives and the friends that were considered close.

She did seem to be trying to include her as part of the family. Randolph Ord, pale and withdrawn, sat in his wheelchair staring out the window. March knew this would be an opportunity to talk to him alone. Perhaps the only chance he'd get.

"Mr. Ord, let me offer my deepest sympathy again," March said, extending his hand. Mr. Ord took it but showed no signs of knowing who March was. "Sandy March, Durango PD. I spoke with you and your wife earlier about Randy's death."

Recognition brightened the dark eyes and then faded again. He let March's hand slip from his.

"Sit, if you'd like," Randolph said pointing to the window seat in front of him. "If only he would have come home..." His voice trailed off.

March could sense that Mr. Ord knew much more about Randy than he had let on in his previous visit and he waited.

Finally, Randolph Ord told him of his visits to Randy that he was sure neither Ruth nor Beatrice knew about. He told March about his help in getting Randy an interview at the Colorado Mining and Engineering Firm. Ord's eyes hardened when he spotted Ruth and a man March recognized as Joe "PaPa" Belongi, a major crime family boss. Ord turned his wheelchair abruptly and made his way out of the room without looking back, not even a final word to March.

March tried to work his way over to Ruth and Belongi without being conspicuous. Ruth turned and straightened up when she saw him.

"So sorry about your brother," Belongi said.

"Mr. March, I see you brought the new Mrs. Ord to survey the kingdom," she said acidly. "Don't know if you know Joseph Belongi. He's a friend of the family, goes way back. Mr. Belongi, this is Detective Sandy March of the Durango PD." She hammered down on the word *detective*, March felt, to send a red flag to Belongi. March already knew Belongi and he was sure Belongi knew him. PaPa Belongi had a long list of indictments. Unfortunately, he was never convicted on any of the charges. He was head of an organized crime family that held grip on at least a fourth of Colorado. Someday he would trip, do something that would crumple his empire. Yes, March knew him and he knew March. He had become something of a nemesis to Belongi.

Belongi extended his hand. "Ah, yes Mr. March. You're a long way from home aren't you?"

"Doing a friend a favor," March said shaking Belongi's fat, sweaty hand. "Wanted to extend my condolences again Ms. Ord," he said turning to Ruth.

"Thank you. Could you excuse me? I need to see how father is doing," she said, leaving Joe Belongi and March to struggle effecting polite conversation for as long as they could tolerate each other. March excused himself finally by saying there was someone else he needed to talk to.

March looked around trying to find Danielle. He saw her coming out of a huge mahogany doorway. She had left the door open and Beatrice stood in the middle of the room with a look on her face he couldn't describe. Danielle rushed through the crowd and out the front door before March could catch up to her.

"Danielle," he called as he saw her running down the long driveway. "Danielle, wait."

Danielle was running because Beatrice Ord had offered to buy Danielle's baby. All she had to do was say yes and she could come and live with them until the baby was born. He'd have the best medical care and she would have the best of everything. They would give her enough money to get settled, until she could get a job, somewhere back in Wisconsin where she belonged. All she had to do was sign a paper Beatrice had her lawyer draw up, in effect giving up all rights to ever see the child after it was born.

"I hate that woman! How dare she think she could buy my baby? How dare she think I am the kind of person who would sell a tiny, helpless baby? If the way she raised Randy is any example of the way she would raise my son, I'd rather he be dead then let her raise him." Danielle's eyes told the story if her voice didn't. There was a fire in them that March had not seen before. "Let's get the hell out of here before I do something I'll regret," she said with a new courage and conviction March enjoyed seeing.

"We're on our way little lady," he said, shutting the car door after she got in.

"First Ruth, now Beatrice—they think money can buy anything. Well, I'll show them. No wonder Randy wanted nothing to do with them. No wonder he kept them a secret. He must have been ashamed of them and their almighty money worship."

She threw her hat with the little veil into the back seat. She opened the backpack on the floor and said, "Close your eyes I need to get comfortable. Well, maybe you better not close them seeing as how you're driving, but keep them on the road, will you please?" She smiled and March knew she would be okay. Ruth or Beatrice would not break this feisty little cat.

"Will do," he said. "But you know you're asking an awful lot of a mortal man."

"Well, if you don't want to end your stay on this planet, I'd suggest you keep your eyes on the road." With that she pulled the little black dress over her head and dove into a red sweatshirt. She squirmed into a pair of Levi's

"What will the neighbors, I mean the other drivers, think?" he teased.

"Hey if they don't watch TV, they have never seen a woman get dressed. If they do, they will just be jealous that they haven't the guts to be so bold."

The drive back to Durango showed March a whole new side of Danielle Maynard Ord. He liked this girl more than ever.

He found out that Ruth had offered to pay her to have an abortion and she also offered to buy her plane fare back to her aunt's in Wisconsin. Danielle was furious that Ruth had checked her out. Even finding out about her roots in Wisconsin. She was even more furious about her offer.

It was late when they arrived back at JC's apartment.

"Want to come in for coffee?"

"No, better not," he said reluctantly. "I've really got a heavy day tomorrow. The DA wants some answers about Randy's death. Apparently, the senior Ords are putting pressure on him to get it solved."

"The Ord money again," she said. "Thanks for taking me to the funeral, Mr. M—I mean Sandy." She stood on tiptoe and kissed his cheek. Before he could react she was inside and closed the door.

"Whew," he blew out to the crisp night air. "And I'm supposed to sleep tonight?" He shook his head and got in his car.

Thirty-four

Danielle used her back to push the heavy metal door to the alley open as she struggled with the heavy garbage bag. This was the one part of her job she didn't like. The alley was always so dark and she never knew when the homeless people from the neighborhood would be rummaging. Not that she was afraid of them exactly, but she worried that. . . well, some of them were winos and she heard they could be pretty aggressive at times.

The garbage cans lined the wall of the building. The contents of one can were spilled all over the ground around it. It had to be the work of a trash picker because she always made sure the lids were down tight. Lifting the lid to the nearest can, she picked up the bag. An engine revved down the alley and headlights blinded her when she looked to see where they were coming from.

The car careened toward her. There was nowhere to go. Nowhere to run. It was going to hit her. She heard herself scream and felt the crushing blow that sent her flying into the air and down on the hood of the car. The slide off the fender when the driver slammed on the brakes dropped her to the pavement and the car sped away. Struggling to lift her head, all she could see were red taillights. The pain in her back and left arm forced another scream from her raw throat. Warm liquid oozed from the back of her head before the whole world went black.

The next thing Danielle knew she awoke to the bleak whiteness of a hospital room with machines beep beeping and bright lights glaring all around her.

Thirty-five

JC answered the door in an over-sized flannel shirt and leggings. It made March think of some castaway waif in an old movie.

"Come in, Mr. March," she said backing up and holding the door for him to enter. "Please have a seat. Can I get you a drink, anything?" She made nervous hand gestures that swept the room.

"No, nothing. I'm fine," March said almost afraid to enter the stark whiteness of the room. The total white décor was accented only with touches of black and a single red rose in a black bud vase on the glass top dinning table. Precariously, he sat on a black leather barstool at the kitchen breakfast nook. He cleared his throat tentatively." Ms...Smythe—"

"Please, it's JC."

"Ah, JC, there is no easy way to ask this question so I'll just ask it because I have to. You knew about the candle that Danielle made to get rid of Randy, right?"

JC nodded her agreement, nervously. "But, you knew that. Danielle said she told you about it. But I didn't light the candle,"

"Right. Okay, JC, so Randy was already dead before you lit the candle, because the autopsy showed there was no cyanide in his system. I could, however, have you prosecuted for attempted murder. You realize this, don't you?" March looked at JC with a scowl on his face that hid his true sympathy for the girl.

He didn't know if the bluff would work, but she was the only one who could have lit the candle. Thelma was not around; she was off trucking with Horn when Randy Ord was murdered. JC was the only other person who knew about the candle. Also, the lab said the matchbook had three sets of fingerprints. Two unidentified, but they got three good matches with Shorty Delegano. Perhaps she was just trying to help her friend out of a bad situation, but it was against the law no matter what the motive. He needed to be sure she understood the gravity of her actions. Hopefully she would tell all and he could get on to finding the real murderer. Tears threatened to spill over the lower lids of JC's incredibly emerald green eyes as she nodded her head.

"Of course I understand. You don't understand what that animal was doing to Danielle. Despite his monstrous acts, she still loved him. I couldn't stand by and watch her suffer any longer. I'm really sorry. I know it was wrong. I just didn't see any other alternative, with Danielle expecting his child. I knew that she would go back to him if he asked her, and that she and the baby would both probably wind up dead. I couldn't let that happen. Don't you see?

"I-I snuck over there in the middle of the night to confront Randy. The door was ajar. He was sound asleep and the damn candle was just sitting there on the nightstand. So, I, well, damn it!. He deserved to die. He was such a jerk. What he did to Danielle was unthinkable. So, I lit the candle. That's why you found my fingerprints on the matchbook cover. I really didn't know he was already dead. How could I know? The fan was going. He was laying there. It was way hot in that apartment."

Now the tears flooded the eyes that pleaded with him to understand her dilemma.

"I know how terrible it looked. There are ways of handling these things you know, without resorting to murder," he said, not giving her an inch of sympathy; he didn't dare. He knew the law and he knew the jeopardy in which she had placed herself.

"Oh sure, and a restraining order would what? Stop him from seeing Danielle and making her life miserable. She worked in a public place. She couldn't avoid him in a town this size. Besides, I've read in the papers about dead women who did have restraining orders in place. I did what I had to do. I'm not proud of it. I just did it." JC wiped her eyes with the tissue March handed her.

"I want you to know we are not going to press charges, only because you didn't actually cause his death and you have no prior record. But, please don't ever think you can take the law into your own hands again, promise?"

The telephone interrupted her answer.

"It's for you Mr. March," JC said handing March the phone

"Yo, March here."

"I have a patch through from a State Patrol Officer. He's downtown." March recognized the voice as belonging to Anaheim, the police dispatcher.

"Okay Ann, patch him through."

"Hold on a sec, sir."

"March, Pete Bolstrom here. Hey, you've been working on this Randy Ord thing right?"

"Yeah?"

"Well, his little lady Danielle, we're scraping her up off the alley. Some yo-yo thought taking out the trash cans in the alley behind The Office Bar & Grill looked like a fun past-time. Thought you'd want to come take a look-see. The girl is in pretty rough shape. Guess she was taking out some garbage when it happened."

March felt the blood drain from his face as he listened. "I'm on my way." He grabbed his coat before realizing JC was still sitting there. "Danielle has been in an accident. I don't have any details. Come on, I'm going right over to the scene."

"Oh my God! Who? How?" JC blurted out as she turned to follow March.

"All I know is she was hit by a car in the alley behind the restaurant. Don't know anything else." March raced from the apartment, his heart pounding.

Before JC could get her seat belt on, the car was in motion. March hit the siren and lights as he sped through traffic. A black and white, lights flashing, blocked the entrance to the alley. The ambulance parked face-to-face with the squad car. He pulled his car in at an angle between the squad and the ambulance. The uniformed police officers held back the growing crowd while the emergency crew worked over the unconscious body of Danielle Ord. March pushed his way through, showing his badge. He waved the uniform officer off as he tried to hold JC back. "She's with me," he shouted at the officer. "What happened?"

"Near as we can figure, she was taking trash out from the restaurant. Someone came down the alley and clipped her. There's no skid marks. Doesn't look like they tried to stop. They sped away according to that man over there. He's the one who called it in."

March turned to see an older man with a mop of uncombed gray hair leaning against the building by the restaurant door.

"That's Mack, our cook," JC said as she started toward the man. "Mack, Mack! What happened?"

March was at her side as she introduced him. The man was visibly shaken. "Can you tell us what happened?"

"I heard the garbage cans clattering all over the alley and I knew Danielle was out here, so I hurried out to investigate. There she was, sprawled on the pavement, garbage everywhere. It's awful, plain awful," he said, his voice shaking.

"Did you see the car?" March asked, notebook in hand.

"Yeah, I saw a white car, a big, newer model job. It was a Cadillac I believe, or something ritzy like that."

"You didn't happen to glimpse the license plate number did you?"

"Nah, didn't hardly see the car. They were racing out of here like the devil was hot on their tail. I didn't see no plate— nothing 'cept poor little Danielle lying there like a dishrag. I raced in and called 9-1-1. What else could I do? I ain't no doctor or nothing," Mack said, his head low.

"You did the right thing Mack. One other thing, could you tell who or how many people were in the car?"

"It had those blasted dark windows. I couldn't see a thing. When it hit the street the light coming in through the windshield, I would say there were two people in the car, though. Or, maybe it was those blasted head rest things they put in all the cars now-a-days."

"Thanks. That's all we need for now. I'll probably be contacting you later to come down and give us a statement."

"Is it okay for me to go back to cooking now? There was a restaurant full of people before all this started," Mack said wiping his face on the apron he still wore.

"Sure, sure you go ahead."

The ambulance technicians had Danielle on the stretcher and were ready to transport her when March finished talking to Mack. JC was at her friend's side.

"I'm going with her," JC said as March approached.

"I'll follow in the squad car. I need to ask a few more questions here first," he said to JC. Then he turned to the EMTs. "What's the prognosis?" he asked, fearing the worst.

"She's in pretty bad shape, but I think she'll be okay. We'll know more when she regains consciousness, but her vitals are good and strong."

"Thanks, go ahead, get going," he motioned to them, putting his hand on JC's shoulder. "I'll be there shortly."

She nodded and headed toward the ambulance with the EMTs. March turned around and looked up the alley. Five garbage cans lay with their contents spilled out over the pavement. Blood pooled where Danielle's head had been. The garbage can closest to that spot had a large dent in it. Pete Bolstrom came across the alley to stand next to March.

"Sure doesn't look like they tried to avoid her. I mean the cans were back against that wall there, plenty of room for the trash trucks to get through. Heck even the semis that unload supplies get by. This alley is plenty wide. They didn't need to hit her. Looks deliberate to me." He glanced up at March who seemed to be far away.

"Be sure forensics gets paint samples from this," he said pointing to the dent in the garbage can with flakes of white paint in it. "Talk to anyone who may have seen anything. I'll get Lesh down here and you can canvas the apartments on both sides of this alley. I am going to the hospital."

Thirty-six

March walked into the hospital room. Machines chirped and gurgled, lives suspended by the umbilical cords connected to mechanical monsters that beeped and burped the history of every heartbeat, every breath of air. It was eerie and put his nerves on a knife's edge, and cut a path through to his heart. He knew he should not become involved with a suspect, a victim, a witness, or whatever it was that Danielle should eventually become in the macabre scenario in which he found himself. March saw JC hovering over Danielle in the corner of the large room, a yellow curtain, halfway closed, blocked his view of the patient in the bed but he knew it had to be Danielle.

JC looked up as he entered the room and motioned him to the bedside.

"Hi, March, I'm glad to see you," she said in a barely audible whisper.

March saw the pale figure resembling a mannequin tied to tubes and cords and machines. He felt his knees grow weak. This vibrant, troubled young woman he wanted to love and protect seemed a breath away from leaving him. He reached out with a shaky hand to caress the small frail hand boarded to an intravenous bottle. She felt cold and clammy, not alive, not pulsing with life. He fought to keep back the tears he felt being dragged from his heart to his eyes.

"How is she? I got here as soon as I could," he managed to get past the lump in his throat.

"They think she'll be fine. She is pretty bruised up. They found a couple cracked ribs but didn't find any broken bones. They're worried she may lose the baby though. They have her heavily sedated hoping to keep her quiet until morning."

A nurse entered to take Danielle's vital signs. "You'll have to leave," she said to March and JC.

"Can you tell me how she's doing? I'm Sandy March, a detective from the Durango PD."

"I'm sorry, I don't know the particulars. You'll have to talk to Doctor Spade. He's down the hall at the nurse's station right now."

March and JC left the room, hurrying to the nurse's station to talk to the doctor.

"I am Detective March from the Durango PD. I need to talk to the doctor in charge of Danielle Ord's case," March said to the nurse at the desk.

"Doctor Spade, a detective from the Durango PD wants to talk to you," she said to a tall thin man standing by a file cabinet and going through some charts.

"Let's go into my office," he said motioning to March.

"You stay here, JC. I will be back in a few minutes," he said following the doctor into a small room just off the nurse's station.

"Detective March, how can I be of help? I was told this was a hit and run."

"Yes, that's right doctor. I wonder, has Danielle said anything since she was brought in?" He was hopeful that she was at least conscious, that would give him hope that her recovery would be swift.

"No, I'm afraid she was unconscious when she arrived. We didn't find any concussion though so the prognosis is good. There are no broken bones, no internal injuries. She's a lucky young lady. One problem though—she may lose the child she's carrying. Judging from the bruises on her body, it appears that she went over the hood of the car. She's really lucky not to be more seriously injured."

"Any idea when I will be able to get a statement from her?" March asked.

"It won't be until morning. I thought it best to sedate her pretty heavily in hopes the rest will keep her from losing the baby."

March gave the doctor his home telephone number as well as the precinct number and told him to call him if there was any change. The doctor agreed.

"We may as well leave, JC. There won't be anything we can do tonight. They expect her to sleep until morning. If you like, I could drop you back home."

"That would be nice if you're sure we shouldn't stay just in case she wakes up or takes a turn for the worse," JC said, tears in her eyes.

"No, I gave the doctor my home number, He'll call me if anything changes. If he does, I'll call you right away. Promise."

"Who would do such a thing? Why Danielle? She never hurt anyone."

"I don't know. Maybe it was just an accident. A reckless driver or maybe someone with a few too many. We'll be doing further investigating of course, just in case it wasn't an accident. I can't imagine it wasn't just a freak thing," March said trying to console JC, but he had his doubts. He didn't believe it was an accident. Something in his gut told him it was deliberate.

Once in the car, JC burst into tears. March looked at her thinking it was her friend's condition that brought on the tears. Suddenly she blurted out

"Mr. March, I'm the one who lit the cyanide candle in Randy's apartment. It wasn't Danielle. She told me she had made it. She told me she planned to light it. I-I just couldn't stand to see her suffer any more at the hands of that brute. I thought no one would ever know. I never expected anyone to suspect Danielle. I don't know what I was thinking. I'm sorry, I'm so sorry. Now this, hasn't Danielle suffered enough. If she loses that baby, it will kill her. Even though he brutalized her, she loved him dearly. She wanted their child more than anything in the world."

March did not want to hear that Danielle loved Randy. He did need to hear that she was not the one who had lit the candle, because although it did not cause Randy's death, which he knew now, it was still attempted murder. Since he and JC had just gone over her involvement, he knew she must be feeling very guilty and the pain of her friend's predicament caused the outburst. She was looking for absolution for what she had done and he was now prepared to offer her the sympathy she so desperately needed.

"I know, JC, and we've been all over that. It wasn't your fault. He was dead before you got there. Danielle knows this and she loves you for being her friend for trying to help her. She would never blame you for what happened to Randy. We will find out who did it. So dry those tears and just be there for Danielle when she needs you, because she will after this."

"Okay, I just feel so lousy for her. What if she loses that baby she wants so desperately?"

"We will deal with that if it happens. Right now Danielle is our only concern and finding out who did this to her." He dropped JC off at her apartment and went home himself. Hoping if he slept on it, he would find some answers. If he could sleep that is.

He was not sure what to do next.

Thirty-seven

"According to all the witnesses we talked to, no one saw the car. They heard the crash of garbage cans, but they didn't see what it was," Lesh said.

"Someone has to have seen something. There are a dozen apartments above the businesses in that area there must be at least one person who saw something," March said to his partner. "Let's go door to door on both sides of the alley. That's the only hope we have unless Danielle Ord can tell us something when she wakes up."

"Why don't we just give her time to do that?" Lesh asked, shaking his head.

"Because in that amount of time, memories fade, and our driver could be in the next state that's why."

"Don't suppose it would have anything to do with your feelings about our Ms. Ord, would it?" Lesh asked.

"Enough already. We investigate crime. That's what we get paid for. It doesn't have to be anything personal. Now let's get with it. We've got a lot of doors to knock on," March said grabbing his jacket off the back of his chair.

Maybe I do care what happens more than in most cases, but I still do things by the book, March thought as he left the office with his partner.

They had canvassed the entire block. No one had seen or heard anything unusual. March was beginning to think the town was becoming more like the metropolis of Denver everyday. No one ever saw or heard anything. They would turn their heads if it meant they had to become involved in anything. "New York mentality" he called it. An old man, bent and shaky, answered the door of another apartment. It faced the alley; it had windows that looked down into and across the street at the same type of tall brick building. The same view, businesses below, apartments above. The old man looked at their badges though glasses that he had to cock to read through.

"Come on in, young fellers," he said, his voice cracking like an old gramophone record. His apartment was a museum of a life he had lived—even the furniture though antique to March, was probably from his era. "Would you gentlemen like a cold drink? I have some tea in the icebox."

"No, thank you. We would like to ask you some questions about an accident that happened in the alley last night," March said.

"You know, I figured someone would be around. Those tires screeching, garbage cans flying every which way. Some one got hurt, didn't they?" he asked, lowering himself into an overstuffed chair.

"As a matter of fact someone did," Lesh said looking out the window at the alley below. "Right there across from your window, behind The Office Bar & Grill."

"Did you see anything? Perhaps the car that did the screeching?" March asked.

"Well, I heard the commotion, so I hurried over to the window. I was doing dishes at the time so it took a minute to get there. But I did see taillights headed down the alley."

"Could you describe the car?" March asked hopefully.

"I couldn't say for sure. All those new cars look alike. I do believe it was a light color. Maybe white or light blue."

"Can you tell us anything else, a license plate number maybe?"

"No, these old eyes don't see that good, Detective. It was a rental. You know how they always have those stickers on the plates. That much I did see. Can't tell you which place. Believe it was the Hertz logo though, near as I can tell. It was a light car. One of those expensive ones like a Caddy, maybe, or a big Buick. I'm just not sure."

"Did you see the driver, or notice how many people were in the car?"

"When they hit the street, the light shined though the windows but I couldn't make it out—maybe the driver was wearing a hat. But, no I didn't see any faces. Sorry."

"If you think of anything else, no matter how inconsequential it may seem, would you give me a call down at the station? Here's my card," March said. "Thank you for your time."

"Was I any help at all? Back in the old days, I would have been down on the street helping that young woman in a flash. I just don't get around the way I used to," he said with a note of sadness in his voice.

"You were the most help we've gotten so far. We really appreciate it. Thanks," March said.

The old man opened the apartment door for them. March noticed the lock system. Dead bolts, the old slide locks, and security chains made it look like they were leaving Fort Knox. "Do you have much trouble with break-ins around here?"

"The riff-raff that hangs around these buildings, I'm not taking any chances," the old man said. "We have homeless people sleeping in the stairwells every night. You never know when some druggie is going to try to break in."

"I understand," said March. "Better to be safe then sorry."

"You got that right. Good luck, detectives, in finding them guys."

When they reached the street March had another idea. "We haven't thought to question some of the homeless people who regularly sleep in these alleyways and doorways," he said to Lesh.

"We could get a couple of the undercover guys to walk the neighborhood tonight. Maybe they could turn up something," Lesh said.

"Sounds like a good idea to me," March said.

"Let's go talk to Karen Best. I got a message this morning that she is finally home again," March said as he put the blue sedan in gear.

Thirty-eight

"Ms. Best, I'm Detective Sandy March with the Durango PD. This is my partner Gordy Lesh. We're investigating a homicide that occurred two weeks ago in your building. Actually, right across the hall from you. Randy Ord was found dead in his bed at the apartment across from you. Did you know him?"

"How horrible! No, Mr. March, I didn't know him. I had seen him several times, but I never actually knew him beyond saying hello in the hallway."

"Do you remember anything unusual happening on the evening of September fourteenth? That was the day the coroner says he died."

He could almost see the wheels turning in her head as Karen Best thought. "That was almost a month ago. Just before I went to see my daughter in Phoenix. I have been gone since then. I would have to think about that. It was the day before I left. See I work nights, cleaning offices. I usually get home around two or three in the morning. The only thing I can say for sure is that the homeless woman was sleeping in the hallway downstairs."

"Homeless woman?"

"Yes, she told me her name once. It was Blanche something—ah...Sternwood? No...no that's not right. Stewart?

That's it. Blanche Stewart. I haven't seen her since I've been back. I'm not surprised though. In our conversations she revealed to me she was a graduate student, studying the life of a homeless woman for a paper she was doing."

"Do you have any idea what school? Maybe she saw something that could help us."

"I believe she said the University of Colorado in Denver." Best said. "Wait, now that I think about it I do remember three men in suits at Ord's door when I came home that night. I thought it was strange then because of the lateness and the suits. The crowd that visited there didn't wear suits."

"Can you describe the men?"

"No, I don't think so. It was so long ago. I do remember one other thing though. That night there was a white Cadillac parked outside. Another thing that doesn't fit in this neighborhood."

"Thank you Ms. Best. That may give us a little more to go on. Here's my card. If you think of anything else, anything at all, even if you think it's trivial, call me at that number."

"I will, Mr. March. I'm sorry I can't be of more help," she said, opening the door.

Back at Headquarters, Sandy March waited on the phone line for Student Records to look up Blanche Stewart's class schedule. They said she was a graduate student working off campus on her master's thesis involving the homeless population, particularly women.

"Mr. March. Blanche Stewart is scheduled to have a conference with her advisor on October fifteenth. I could put a note in her file to get in touch with you. We have no other way of contacting her," said the female voice on the other end of the line.

"I guess that will have to do. Does she have any family or friends that you know of that would be in contact with her on a regular basis? Perhaps someone we could contact before that date? This is an urgent police matter. We think she may have some valuable information that we could use."

"I don't see anything in her records that would indicate she has any family at all. As for friends, working on her own the way she is, I don't think that would be relevant either. I'm sorry we can't be of more help, sir."

"Okay, thanks. If by some odd chance she does contact the school, would you tell her to call Sandy March at the Durango Police Department, please?" As he hung up March pondered the likelihood of her being able to shed any light on the investigation anyway. March got out a stack of index cards and started writing what he knew and what he suspected on them. He lined them up under the people contact headings and then started to rearrange them according to possible motive. Nothing jumped out at him, except Shorty Delegano kept sending up a red flag in his mind.

"Gordy," he called to his partner. "What information did we get on the back ground check on Shorty Delegano?"

Gordy Lesh brought him a thick file. "This man has been involved in a lot of petty stuff. He's got a rap sheet the length of your arm. He's even been the prime suspect in a number of strong-arm deals in Chicago. No convictions ever held up though. Either he leads a charmed life or he is just a little fly making busy for some big boys."

"Maybe this time he overstepped his bounds. Let's go talk to him again. He seemed a little nervous that last time when we ran into him at Randy's friend's apartment."

March no sooner sat down at his desk again than there was a tapping at his door.

He looked up as the woman entered. She was a slim thirtish looking woman with long, rich auburn hair. Her eyes were the blue of a Colorado sky, vivid and sparkling with life and laughter. He was immediately impressed as any male would be unless he was not into woman and March definitely was.

"Mr. March?"

Her voice had a deep baritone that only emphasized her sexuality and attractiveness to March.

"Yes, come in," he said rising from his chair to go to the door.

"I'm Blanch Stewart. Mrs. Best told me you were looking for me. I'm the homeless woman," she laughed. "I guess I better explain that part first. I'm really not homeless. I'm working on my master's thesis in psychology. Broadly speaking, my topic is homeless women in the American west. I am doing research."

"I see," said March feeling like a schoolboy at a loss for words. "Ah, do come in. Here have a seat. Can I get you coffee? Soda? Anything?" He could feel himself blushing. Was it his thoughts that embarrassed him or this woman?

"Coffee would be great," she bubbled as she studied the office and March from head to toe, increasing the color he felt rising from somewhere beneath his navel. "How can I be of help?" she asked after he handed her a cup of coffee.

"Let me pull up my notes," he said, turning to the computer on his desk. "On September fourteenth, were you sleeping in the doorway of the apartment building above the bakery over on Main Street?"

"Let's see, I have my little journal right here," she said pulling a burgundy loose-leaf five by six-inch notebook from her purse. "Yes...yes I was. I made some very specific notes that night. It seems apartment 2A had a lot of visitors late that night."

"That would be what I'm interested in—anything you can tell me about that night."

"Well, I remember very well the three men in suits. They just didn't fit into the area. They arrived in a white Cadillac as I remember. All three were in suits. The short one's suit appeared tailored but the other two were off the rack. The two men in the Wal-Mart suits were huge. They reminded me of gorillas with shaves. The short one seemed to be the boss or leader. They didn't stay long, maybe twenty minutes, a half-hour at the most. Can't tell you any more about them."

"Do you think perhaps you would recognize them if I showed you some pictures?" he asked.

"I might, though with that dim hallway light, I can't promise you anything."

"We'll give it a try before you leave, that is if you can spare the time," he said hoping she could. He would enjoy having her around in the dingy atmosphere of the police precinct, and she was like a ray of sunshine. He felt himself blush again. What was the matter with him anyway? He was acting like an idiot. She didn't seem to notice. She was busy looking in the small notebook.

"Did you see or hear anyone else come or go?" he asked.

"You know about Karen Best, let's see. There was a small young woman that I had seen many times before. I believe she was the man's wife/girlfriend from what Karen told me. She came after the men left. I'd say an hour later. She didn't stay but maybe five minutes. I thought it strange that she didn't bring anything in or take anything out with her. Maybe she just went to talk to her husband. She didn't stay long enough to do that either, though.

"About forty-five minutes after she left another young woman appeared. She seemed very nervous. I remember she listened at the door for a few minutes before she actually went inside. She was there maybe three minutes. She flew out of there like her tail was on fire." She closed her notebook. "Those are the only people that were there on September fourteenth that I saw and I was there from about midnight until sunrise, say 6:00 a.m. or so."

"Would you mind if I made a copy of your journal?" March asked.

"No, go right ahead. Actually, I won't need it. You can keep it if you want," Stewart said handing the journal across the desk. Her hand lingered longer than it needed to when it touched his.

March pulled out the picture JC gave him when he interviewed her. It was of JC and Danielle together. He had asked her if he could hold on to it until they completed their investigation. She agreed. He now showed it to Ms. Stewart. "Could either of these be the young women you saw that night?" he asked, passing the photograph to her.

"They are, both of them are. The one on the left is his wife, or at least the one I saw there on several other occasions. They used to fight a lot. He knocked her around regularly. I wondered why she would put up with it, poor kid. The other one I only saw that once. Like I said, she seemed in a dreadful hurry when she left that night. Do you think they had anything to do with Mr. Ord's murder?"

"It's possible. We are still working on all the evidence. There isn't much to go on. Your observations will help a lot. At least we can establish who may have seen him alive that night."

"I wouldn't blame her, Mrs. Ord that is, if she did help him leave this world. She worked nights while he partied, and then beat her around when she came home. It was not something that would encourage me to come home every night."

"People put up with a lot in the name of love," he said taking back the photo from her. "Would you look at this sheet of mug shots and tell me if you see any of our three men from that night?"

Stewart studied the photos. "There," she said tapping a mug shot of a balding man who looked a lot like Don Rickles. "That's the one in the tailored suit. I'm sure of it, I remember thinking at the time, I never did like Don Rickles, and this man is his double. I don't see—wait, here's another one...this man right here. He was one of the other ones. I don't see the third man though."

"Thanks. This will be a great help. A really great help," March said taking back the sheet of mug shots.

"Is there anything else I can do?" she asked, smiling up at him as she stood beside him.

"Not right now. But, if you think of anything else give me a call will you?"

"Sure I will. If you have any more questions, or whatever," she scrawled a phone number on a piece of paper and handed it to March, "here's my phone number. If I'm not there, leave a message. I have no tie-downs so I don't spend a lot of time there. I do check my messages every day though, so feel free." She winked and turned to go.

March opened the door for her and his senses picked up the berry scent of freshly washed herbal hair shampoo. He watched as she threaded her way through the maze of desks in the outer office. Several heads turned to watch her walk through. She definitely had a presence about her, he thought, as he slowly closed the door.

The Homeless Blanch Stewart's journal was written in the third person, as stories, with her words spoken or unspoken in quotes. March studied the entries of September fourteenth with interest.

Midnight September 14:

"In my usual place in the stairwell of the bakery building: Visitors—three men in suits arrive in a white Cadillac."

The woman settled into her favorite sleeping spot in the enclosure below the apartments just off Main Street where she liked to spend the nights. By 2:00 a.m., the only interruption would be the cleaning lady who sometimes brought her soup and would sit and chat with her while she ate it. She had promised the next time there was an opening in the company that she worked for she would put in a good word for Blanch. She was a lovely woman, seemed to be hard working and alone.

The three men stepped over the homeless woman like they thought she was passed out drunk. They didn't see her peer at them through sleepless eyes. They didn't hear her thoughts as she assessed their appearance and their motive for being at this particular address at this particular time of night. They didn't hear the wheels of her mind churning and recording as though some one had pushed the save button on a computer. But, she was filing away the details, as was her habit both as a writer and a journalist. Blanch Stewart had a mind like a camcorder, she could write the episodes for Murder She Wrote.

She watched as the white Cadillac squealed away from the curb and headed down Main Street. She pulled a small journal from her pocket and sketched in the notes to her imagined tale. Then she curled up and tried once more to sleep.

Visitor: 1:38 a.m. "Young wife of man in apartment 2A. Strange time for a visit. First she's been home in a week. Interesting. She donated $5 to my tin cup. Such a sweetheart."

Blanch Stewart's reminiscence was interrupted by a tiny young woman who cautiously tiptoed around her and made her way up the stairway. Blanch recognized her as the wife of the man in apartment 2A. She disappeared behind the door of the apartment. Blanch curled up and closed her eyes again. Suddenly the young woman came flying down the stairs. She paused briefly by Blanch and took a five-dollar bill out of her pocket, "Bless you," she whispered. "There but for the grace of God go I." With that she was out the door and gone. "Strange goings on in this place tonight," Blanch said to her journal as she made a hasty note. She tucked the five dollars into her pocket and rearranged her clothes to try again to sleep.

Visitor: 2 a.m. "Another young woman. Haven't seen this one before. She too has stopped at apartment 2A. Busy night for that little apartment. Shhh. Here she comes."

Blanch was about to doze off when a red-headed young woman slithered past her and sneaked up the stairs, listening intently at the door to 2A she slid inside. Moments later she streaked down the stairs and out to the street like someone had lit her tail afire. She gave no notice to the half-open eyes of the homeless woman huddled in the corner.

"Did you see that Angelica?" *she asked, pulling the one-armed little doll from her bag. The much loved doll recovered from a trash barrel had one arm missing, disheveled brown hair, the face the homeless woman considered the most angelic she'd ever seen. She had rescued her and dressed her in clothes she'd fashioned from various castoffs. She had become her sole companion in a lonely and dangerous world of homeless women.*

"This is by far the most interesting place we've slept in. All sorts of strange visitors to these apartments all hours of the night."

She made notes in the little notebook and hung it around the doll's neck. "You take good care of this Angelica, it may make a good story some day." *She tucked her into her clothes and curled into the corner to dream of what might have been and will be in a world filled with another tomorrow.*

If the boxcars were not so over crowded this time of year she would sleep there, but this time of year all sorts of riff-raff slept there. It was much safer here for a homeless woman of any age.

Thirty-nine

"We've got some interesting developments here," Lesh said plopping himself down in the chair across from March's desk.

"E-Line Trucking?"

"Yeah. Guess who the owner is?"

"Spit it out. I don't have time for twenty questions," March said gruffly.

"Ruth Ord, sole owner. Bought it up about two years ago. General Manager—one Joseph P. Belongi."

March spun around from the black board where he had chalked in the next link in their puzzle of the investigation of Randy Ord's death. "Belongi, as in 'PaPa' Belongi?"

"Down to every slimy letter," Lesh said grinning like the Cheshire cat.

"Randy's friend Horn works for E-Line Trucking. I think I smell an interview about to cook somebody's goose. Danielle said his name was Jamie Casio. Want to go for a ride?" March asked Lesh as he slipped into his shoulder holster and reached for his jacket.

"Also, remember the lab said the match book had three sets of finger prints? Two unidentified, but they got three good matches with Shorty Delegano?" Lesh reminded him in as they drove toward Jamie Casio's apartment.

"Any luck on those paint samples yet?"

"Forensics expected to have the results on your desk this afternoon."

"We'll have Delegano brought in for questioning as soon as we talk to Horn. Really want those paint samples back first. Delegano has a big white Caddie. I suspect our paint samples will match. We have Blanch Stewart and Karen Best placing three men in suits and the white Cadillac at Randy's apartment the night he was killed. But, why would he try to get rid of Danielle? That part doesn't' make any sense, unless..." March parked the car in front of the address he had for Jamie Casio.

The tall blond-haired person that answered the door was one of the men March had seen at the cemetery wearing the E-line Trucking uniform. Now he had on Levi's and nothing else.

"Jamie Casio?"

"Yeah, who are you?"

"I'm Sandy March, Durango PD. This is my partner, Gordy Lesh. Wonder if you'd give us a few minutes of your time?"

"Ah, sure, come on in," he said backing out of the way to let them in.

They were right about the "horn" part March thought looking at the Jimmy Durante nose. "You were friends with Randy Ord. Is that correct?"

"Guess you could say that," he said cautiously as he looked from him to Lesh and back again. He motioned to the couch, "Sit if you want."

"Thanks." March scanned the modestly furnished clean apartment. "Did Randy drive a semi for E-Line?"

Horn looked like he was scrambling for a way to avoid the question. "Well, ah...is that what Danielle said?" he asked.

"Not exactly. However, we know he was driving for someone. Figured since you were friends and all it made sense to be E-Line."

"I, well, yeah, but he wasn't a regular driver. He only drove once in a while when he needed money."

"What does E-Line haul, usually?" Lesh interjected.

"Anything and everything, our broker, Kim Koepecki, gets the loads, we say where and when."

"What do you know about Joseph Belongi?"

"He's the boss."

"Who owns E-Line?"

"God, how the hell should I know? Belongi signs my check that's all I need to know. Maybe he owns it. He's the boss. Why don't you ask him?"

"Maybe we will. Where were you the night Randy was murdered?" March said.

"San Francisco. Thelma and me—she's my old lady, ah, girl friend. We left the day after Randy's last party. You can check my DOT books. We got back the day before the funeral. Hell, man, you don't think I had anything to do with Randy's death, do you? He was my friend for Christ's sake." Horn bolted from the chair he was sitting in and began pacing.

"No one said you had anything to do with it. We're just looking for clues to what might have happened," March said. "Who was the other driver I saw you with at the cemetery?"

A look of confusion and recognition came over Horn as he dug for the right answer. "Mace, ah Mace Adleback. He and I hung together. Sometimes we'd party with Randy. Usually, though he stayed pretty much away from the parties. He's a loner. Sometimes we had loads going in the same direction, so we would travel together, keeping each other company."

March made a mental note. Mace Adleback was the man Blanche Stewart fingered from the mug shots.

"Was he with you during the San Francisco run?" Lesh asked.

"No, he drew a short haul down to Mexico. He was probably back the next day."

"Do you know where we can find him?" March asked.

"He has a place over on LaPlatta Avenue off Second Street. Number 43, I guess the number is."

"Okay, thanks for your help," March said, standing to leave.

"I can't believe anyone would kill Randy. He was a good guy and a hell of a friend," Horn said walking the men to the door.

Horn couldn't offer them much more but March was happy with what they had gotten. They drove over to Mace Adleback's address. A white Cadillac was pulling away from the curb while they were still a block away.

"Delegano?" Lesh asked.

"Could be, with a truck driver? Let's hang back and see where they go. We can question Adleback later," March said.

They kept a safe distance behind the white Cadillac. When they turned into E-Line Trucking, March kept going down the block.

"What do you suppose?" Lesh left the question hang in the air.

"A connection between Belongi and Delegano? I wouldn't be surprised," March said. "I need the answer to those paint samples before we have Delegano picked up and I want him picked up in his car."

"I get it, so we can impound the car and check it out."

"Exactly," March said.

March's beeper sounded. He pulled the radio microphone from its holder. "March to headquarters," he said.

"March, forensics just called and I thought you'd like to know their findings right away," the voice on the other end said.

"Great, what did they find?"

"They found paint on the garbage cans at the scene where Danielle was hit. They say the paint is definitely from a white car, probably a Cadillac because of the color break down."

"White is white, isn't it?" March said.

"I guess not in the auto industry. All companies have their own mix, the way they put the colors together is almost like a signature."

"Thanks, we'll get right on it." He replaced the microphone.

"Interesting," March said. "So who do we know that has a white Cadillac?"

"I don't know, other than Shorty Delegano, but I imagine if there was any damage done to a car like that it would be in a body shop real fast," Lesh said.

"Okay, lets hit the pavement. How many body shops do we have anyway?"

"Three, last I checked," Lesh said. "So I would guess one of them saw it unless of course the owner's from out of the area."

"Don't borrow trouble. Let's just pretend the guy lives around here until after we do the legwork. The way things are stacking up, it could be Shorty Delegano after all," March said, not wanting to think about what they would do if none of the body shops had a white Caddie in lately.

"Yeah, we did have a caddy in here, ah, let's see...when was that?" the body shop owner said flipping through some invoices. "Ah, here it is. Thursday. We had to repair a fender, also replace a headlight."

"Do you have a name and address of the owner?" March asked.

"She paid cash, when she found out the damage estimate, but I do have the license plate number, standard procedure when we work on a car."

"Great. Could you give us that, please?" March asked.

"Something else too. It's a rental job from the Cars 'R Us Automate over on de Rio.

Lesh got back into the sedan. "I can't believe this," he said.

"I'll be damned. Why would she possibly want to hurt Danielle Ord?" March asked, feeling his insides go weak. "We better get a uniform on her hospital door now." March swung the car back around and headed for the hospital.

"I'll call the squad chief right away," Lesh said grabbing the radio microphone from its clip on the dash.

March flipped on the siren and careened down Kerri Avenue, dodging cars, and people as he floored the blue sedan.

Forty

"Danielle? Danielle, can you hear me?"

Danielle realized it was Ruth Ord's voice. "Yes, I can hear you." Danielle thought she said aloud.

"I guess you can't, you little bitch. Good, because you won't be able to hear anything else when I get through with you either. Why couldn't you just let things be? Let Randy destroy himself? No, you had to go marry the derelict. Oh, I know why now. You wanted his kid so you'd get your fingers in the Ord pockets. I worked too hard to let that happen. When daddy goes, it's mine—all mine. I sacrificed my life to play by their rules, to keep their company going, I won't lose it all to some slut. That's all you were to Randy anyway. He's gone through women like most men go through cars. Rides them until they burn out and then he tosses them aside when a shiny new model comes along. You are far from being the first. If you had been smart, you would have left him long ago. Now you *will* leave, not exactly the way you planned but you're gone."

Danielle heard Ruth's heels click across the room. Quietly she shut the door and returned to Danielle's bedside. Ruth slowly pulled the extra pillow from under Danielle's head. She raised it above Danielle.

"Say good-bye, little girl." Ruth lowered the pillow carefully over Danielle's face and pressed down. Danielle didn't resist. She thought she did but she made no outward signs that she knew what was happening.

Danielle was suddenly running down a narrow winding path through the woods. Branches were snatching at her; someone or something was chasing her. Pain was shooting through her lungs but she keeps running. Suddenly, she tripped on a root sticking up in the pathway. She started to fall but never reached the ground. She floated higher and higher into the air. Bright lights hurt her eyes as she was transported higher and higher, vanishing high above the earth. Floating, she looked down on her neighborhood. The houses all reached up trying to grab her. Nothing could reach her.

No one could harm her now. The houses were gross ugly shapes with arms like branches reaching to snag her. She floated higher, away from this dark, ugly atmosphere. Her flowing white night gown billowed around her like a puff of smoke. She felt the cloud setting her down. A mystical green meadow with daisies appeared before her. Fairy children were dancing under a Maypole with gayily colored pastel streamers. They were singing a bright cheerful song. She couldn't make out the words. A black cloud shut out the sun. The children, the valley and the Maypole all shriveled and disappeared. Thistles, blackberry brambles and a knurled old oak tree appeared in their place. A waterfall cascaded over her and all her cares were washed away with the stream. She floated downstream not caring, waving at the other children on the shore. They were shouting at her calling her terrible names, but a shield the words could not penetrate, protected her. She looked up and saw her mother's arms forming the shield around her.

Then her mother waved goodbye.

"Wait, wait for me mom. I miss you. I love you," Danielle screamed. The vision vanished. She felt loss. She felt real pain coming from somewhere outside herself.

~ * ~

"You keep an eye on the entrances," March barked. "If you see Shorty or his two thugs let me know. Follow them up and I'll be waiting." March raced for the elevator. He hammered at the up button, paused a moment, then raced through the door marked "stairs." He climbed the stairs in leaps, his feet barely resting on the steps. The nurses and patients he passed in the corridors looked at him questioningly as he raced to Danielle's room.

Ruth Ord turned as he bolted through the door.

"I-I was just getting her another pillow," she stammered. "Poor thing looks so uncomfortable."

Danielle coughed.

March pushed Ruth aside. "Are you okay Danielle?" he asked.

Danielle coughed again, her eyes opened wide. "I-she..." Danielle gasped.

March turned to Ruth Ord.

"I really must be going. I'll visit again soon sweetie," she said to Danielle.

March turned again to Danielle. She was coughing and gasping—a long drawn-out beep filled the air of the sterile room. March reached for the call button but the room exploded with activity. March didn't see Ruth make a hasty exit. The nurses shoved past March to Danielle.

"Please sir, stand back," a man in white said as he made his way through the confusion to Danielle's bedside.

March stood back and let the doctors and nurses work over Danielle. Soon the machines again gave a rhythmic beep, beep. March took a long breath as the doctor turned to him.

"She's okay now. I think she'll be fine. Something obstructed her air passage and her panic caused things to go haywire for a minute. She's okay. We've sedated her heavily. She needs to rest." The doctor held out his hand. "I am Dr. Benson, the physician on call," he said.

"Sandy March, Durango PD," March said accepting the hand. "I'm investigating the murder of her husband and the accident that put her in here."

"That would be Randy Ord. I read about that in the paper. What happened to Mrs. Ord? Do you think it's connected somehow?"

"I'm beginning to think so. That is why I am here. We want to put a uniformed officer at her door. No one is to go in or out without authorization. Could I count on you to give our officer a list of people who are authorized to see her?"

"Of course. This young woman has seen enough trauma for a while. I'll inform the head nurse right away," he said.

"Thanks Dr. Benson," March said. "Can I talk to her now?"

"Sorry, she's out cold and will be for hours," Dr. Benson said.

March waited until they all left the room. He stood beside Danielle's bed with her pale white hand in his. Something was wrong. Why was Ruth Ord here? Why Danielle's sudden breathing problems. She was doing very well earlier when he called to check on her. He turned as he heard a knock on the door.

Lesh opened it. "The uniform is here," he said.

"Okay, be right out," March said. "Hang in here, little lady," he said as he released her hand.

"No one except her doctor and nurses are to be allowed past this door. Dr. Benson said they would give you a list of the people who are authorized to enter to treat her. No one else, not even a cleaning lady is to get past you. Got that?"

"I understand sir," the officer said taking up a stance in front of Danielle's door.

"Let's get that arrest warrant for Shorty Delegano," March said as he and Lesh walked down the bustling corridor.

On their way to the car, March told Lesh about Ruth Ord's visit and strange behavior. "I think she's connected somehow," he said. "To Randy's death as odd as that seems and to this, too."

"Just because she was in Danielle's room when she had a trauma?"

"No. It's more than that. Danielle seemed to be trying to tell me something about Ruth before all hell broke loose in there," March said feeling very perplexed and helpless. "There is something going on with that woman that involves Danielle, I'm sure."

"She is the sister-in-law you know. Perhaps she's just worried about Danielle and her baby," Lesh said.

"Yeah, you could be right. Let's check out Shorty's car. We know he has a white Cadillac. Maybe his was the one that ran down Danielle. Some how we have to get this thing sorted out before anyone else gets hurt." March said starting up the sedan and backing out of the parking lot.

They drove over to The Italian Restaurant where they knew Shorty's car should be at this time of day. Lesh walked with March around the white Cadillac. There was no evidence of a fresh paint job or any dings or scrapes on it.

"Okay, so it's on to the rental car place, what was it? Cars R something?" March said.

"Cars R us Automate, over on del Rio."

The dispatch office called March. "We have that line up set to go as soon as you can get in here. Ms. Stewart and Ms. Best are already here. What's your 10?"

"We can be there in 5 minutes. Have them wait for us."

"Can do," the voice said.

"Damn, I wanted to check that rental place today. This will set us back, but we need Shorty and any one who can put him at the scene will sure lighten our work load."

"Maybe we won't need to visit the rental place—ever think of that?" Lesh asked.

"Well, we will see about that real quick. Wonder if they had someone pick up Shorty? I can't imagine him volunteering to be in a line-up."

~ * ~

"Okay, thank you both for coming down. Can we have you look at some mug books before you leave? Like to have you try to identify the other two men you saw. Shorty Delegano is the kingpin, but getting the other two would sure speed things up in closing this whole mess."

"Sure, I can do that. What about you, Karen? I'll give you a ride home when we're through?"

"Okay, just point us in the right direction." Karen Best said smiling at Blanche Stewart.

March opened the door and motioned to one of the officers in the outer office. "Take these ladies upstairs. There's a couple mug shot books on my desk. Have them go through them to see if they recognize anyone."

He turned to Lesh, "Let's see if we can get Delegano to tell us anything."

Forty-one

"Mr. March, Mr. Lesh, I believe my client has some information that will make you sit up and take notice. We would like to talk deal." Shorty Delegano's lawyer was a tall, lanky, Abe Lincoln-looking man. March hadn't seen him before. His voice rumbled when he talked.

"Is that a fact, Mr. ah..."

"Muscoli, Abe Muscoli," the lawyer said reaching across the table to shake March's hand. "I'm new around here. Nice little town you've got here though. I could get real used to the laid back life."

"Mr. Muscoli, " March said, thinking how this man seemed to be pumped up on something. "So what is this information that Mr. Delegano thinks I'd be so interested in that I'd be willing to give scum like him a break?"

Muscoli looked at his client and nodded. "Tell the man what you told me."

"I wanna be sure I get out of here first, then I'll talk," Shorty practically whispered to his lawyer, obviously shaken.

"If you've got something good for me, we'll see what we can do about reducing your sentence. Maybe to murder two. You could be out in twenty years or so," March said not feeling in a particularly generous mood. "Besides, that's up to the DA, not me."

"You'll put in a word for me though, right?" Shorty asked in his squeaky asthmatic voice.

"Talk, then we'll deal," March barked at the little worm. He watched as sweat poured down the brow of the pudgy cheeked Delegano.

"Okay, okay. I didn't off Randy Ord. I was there but I didn't do it. It was Mace and Horse. They's the ones who shot him up on heroin. Ruth Ord put up the money to have him wasted and she's the one that wanted Danielle done in, too. But I had nothin to do with the Danielle thing. That was strictly Ruth Ord." The little man squirmed in his seat, his hands nervously clenching and unclenching. "There, there now, you have it all," he said and he slapped the table with his pudgy small fist. He leaned back against the chair and locked his fingers around his rotund belly.

March could not believe his ears. He glanced at Lesh whose face also registered surprise. "Let me get this straight. Ruth Ord paid to have her brother killed, and then tried to kill Danielle herself?"

"Why?" Lesh asked

"How should I know? I don't ask those kinds of questions. I take the money, do the job and that's the end of it."

"How did Ruth Ord find you? And why you?" March asked.

"Hey, the old lady has money. She has connections. How would I know what directory she found my name listed in," wheezed Delegano.

"Don't get cute with me. I need proof. I need some answers," March barked as the little man squirmed in his chair.

"I ain't no dummy, I taped the calls she made to me," Shorty Delegano said.

The lawyer reached in his brief case and produced an answering machine tape. "Got something we can play this on?" He slid the tape across the table to March. March walked over to a cabinet and produced a tape player.

The men listened in silence to the tape. During the first conversation, Ruth tells Shorty who she is, and that she needs to meet with him. In subsequent conversations, she tells him only that she's dissatisfied and does not give her name.

"Maybe we can get a voice match from these. What about the pay-off, was it cash?" March asked.

"Of course, who's going to write a check for a hit," Shorty smirked as he squeezed out the answer. "The large deposit in my bank account will coincide with Randy's death. I deposited it the next day."

"Okay. I'll keep this tape and we'll get back to you as soon as I talk to the DA. I don't know if this will be good enough to convict Ruth Ord of hiring a murder, two murders, or attempted murder in Ms. Ord's case. I'll call you, Mr. Muscoli, as soon as I know."

March turned to Lesh when Shorty and his lawyer were gone. "I guess we better go pick up Ruth Ord."

Lesh nodded and grabbed his jacket from the back of his chair, following his partner out the door.

Forty-two

Ruth left the hospital, driving through the heavy fog that shrouded the mountains like a warm quilt. The fog swallowed the sounds before they expressed themselves; the hissing of her tires in the moisture created by the fog on the roadway mocked her insecurity, her dread of the encounter with her other self. Inside she was Jell-O. Outside she must pretend. She must be all the things they expected her to be.

She found her apartment a comforting haven, a refuge from a world that suddenly had turned on her like some lioness protecting her cubs. The shrill ring of the telephone set off the alarm in her gut that warned her danger was everywhere.

"Thanks, okay, thanks. Damn," Ruth muttered hanging up the phone. That little weasel Delegano. I should have known he'd cave in the minute they squeezed his sleazy hide. Should have known he'd point the finger at me. She was glad that Christy Rutledge worked in the DA's office.

Rutledge always called Ruth with news of the precinct goings on. It paid to wine and dine her. Ruth was always good at using whatever resources were necessary to make things go her way. Her mother had made an excellent teacher for that.

Nervously she paced the white-carpeted living room. If those detectives were just on their way, it would be at least three hours before they arrived. They had a tape Christy said. Damn that Shorty! A clever sleaze-bag to tape their conversations. It was too late to have him erased. Ruth's mind raced through all her possible options turning up dead end after dead end. She didn't dare call Avery. He was a good lawyer, but she doubted even Clarence Darrow could pull enough strings to make this one a walk.

Ruth picked up the gold-framed picture of the happy foursome, the family everyone thought perfect. One boy, one girl, handsome father, beautiful mother, money enough to live happily ever after. *This isn't the way it was supposed to be.* She gently ran her fingers over the faces in the photo.

"I'm so sorry Daddy. I tried to straighten him out, but you and mom—especially you, mother—thought you could buy your way out of everything. He never had to feel the pressure like me. You never expected him to be grown up at five or six. Your precious baby boy was allowed to have a childhood that extended way beyond his eighteenth birthday. It's your fault he's dead. You know it's your fault." She hugged the picture and then flung it into the fireplace. The crash of glass splintered the silence of the decorator-perfect apartment.

Ruth felt her life splintering like the glass in that frame. Slowly she walked into her study and pulled the burgundy desk chair over to the window. The view of the mountains had always given her strength and soothed her longing to be loved or at least appreciated by her parents. She knew then what she must do. She wouldn't, she couldn't face what this scandal would do to her parents. Ruth hated her mother for the way she'd hurt her for so many years. This was one way of getting even, and of paying her back for all those years when Randy got the love she craved.

Opening the gold-handled drawer of the oak desk, "Masculine," she said, "see what I've become, more man—more CEO—than woman," she pulled a sheet of embossed stationery from the drawer. The Victorian elegance she appreciated, turned hard and cold like her. "Harmph—spilled milk!" Pacing, she tried to come up with a way out. Hastily, she went to the bedroom and started tossing things into a suitcase, then stopped, looked in the mirror and flung the half-full suitcase across the room.

"No," she sobbed. "I can't run anywhere. It's too late." She picked up the telephone and dialed Stew Granger's number. He had been the family legal counsel for three decades. He'd know what to do, who to call. "He's where? He won't be...which hospital? I'll send-send a card—thanks. No. No one else. Thank you."

Ruth Ord replaced the phone and hugged herself in pain and realization. There was no out for what she had done. Her parents would never forgive her for what she had done to Randy. This was one mess she would clean up herself and this time there would be no loose ends. A scotch neat would steal her against what she must do; she carried it with her to the study, pulled a piece of stationery from the leather tray and inserted it into the typewriter. After a long slow swallow from the glass of scotch, Ruth began to type. *To whom it may concern:* A pause and another long drink. When she finished the letter, she left it in the typewriter.

She rinsed her glass in the sink and walked slowly through the house. Pausing by the portrait of her and Randy with their parents, she thought about what had prompted this portrait. His high school graduation.

"Always Randy, wasn't it?" she said to the portrait. "I loved you so, and now—" She swiped the tears from her eyes, squared her shoulders and walked down the hall to the master bathroom. Several lavender candles lined the bathtub. She lit them as she filled the tub with water and got undressed, slipped into the tub of hot lavender-scented water.

Forty-three

"We're on our way now. Okay you get the arrest warrant. We'll pick it you up when we hit Colorado Springs. About three hours. Okay see you then." Lesh closed the cell phone and starred out at the blue hues shrouding the mountains. They seemed to relay the mood. "All set," he said to March.

"Good. I can't believe Ruth Ord actually thought she would get away with all this bull shit." He pulled out to pass a semi that had slowed in the middle of the next big hill.

"Whoa, you may be ready to meet your maker, but I'm not," Lesh said grabbing hold of the dashboard.

"Sorry," March said easing up on the accelerator. "I just get so PO'd at the way people think their money makes up for their ignorance."

"I know. But getting us killed sure isn't going to change that, is it?" Lesh released his death grip on the dashboard.

The drive to Colorado Springs was, for the most part, a silent uneventful trip. They pulled up to the police station a little before noon.

George Davis, the sergeant at the desk held out his hand. "Here's the warrant you wanted. Took the liberty of calling her office just to see where we might find her. Her secretary said she already went home for the day. Said she didn't feel well."

"Thanks," March said, taking the warrant from Davis. "We've had a long drive. Think we'll grab a bite to eat before we go over to her apartment."

"Got a couple of blues all set to go with you," Sgt. Davis said.

"Should be routine. Not expecting any trouble from her," March said.

March and Lesh left the police building and headed for a small café. "I don't think there's any hurry to pick her up. Can't see her going anywhere. She's run the company since her father turned ill. We may as well eat. We won't get the chance once we pick her up," March said.

"Sounds good to me," Lesh agreed.

An hour later, March rang the doorbell of Ruth Ord's suite. There was no answer so he rang again. The minutes ticked by. No one came to the door. The desk clerk had said she came in an hour ago and hadn't left. March knocked loudly. "Go get the manager and have him come up here and open this door," March told one of the uniformed officers.

The manager slid the key into the lock and opened the door. "Ms. Ord? Ms Ord, are you decent?" he called as March and Lesh pushed past him and into the suite.

The men canvassed the rooms one at a time. March saw the suitcase lying open, its sides spread like the wings of a wounded bird. Clothes were strewn from the closet to the open suitcase like someone had flung it across the room. Foul play flashed across his mind as he rushed from the bedroom into the living room. Nothing else seemed out of place. Ruth Ord seemed to be gone. March knocked on the closed bathroom door and then opened it, unprepared for the macabre scene he came across.

"Lesh, I found her," he said.

The two men stared at the pool of blood turning the bath water pink. Ruth Ord had slit her wrists.

"Call the coroner and an ambulance," March barked.

March wandered from the bathroom to the study where he found the letter in the typewriter. Ruth Ord confessed to her brother's death and Danielle's accident. She blamed her parents for both incidents.

"I was never good enough and he could never do any wrong, I'm tired of it all." She signed the note *"Remember me, Ruthy"* Beside the note was a cassette tape with the words "The Ticket Home" scrawled on the label.

"Lesh look at this. We hit the jackpot," March called out to his partner. However, the victory didn't taste sweet. They never did. When someone takes their own life the system is robbed of its function—truth—closure—they're all part of a solved case, not suicide, never suicide.

Forty-four

Randolph and Beatrice Ord stood beside Danielle's hospital bed.

"Please Danielle, let us help with the hospital bills. It's the least we can do for the mother of our son's child," Beatrice Ord's smooth voice reminded Danielle of French Vanilla Ice Cream.

"I would appreciate the help, at least until I get back on my feet and can repay you," she said.

Mrs. Ord reached for her hand. "There, there child. Don't you worry about paying us back. We want you to have a healthy child to be heir to the Ord fortunes. We'll gladly pay everything. You needn't trouble yourself. You can come live with us while you're waiting for the baby. What do you say?"

Danielle looked from Randolph to Beatrice, studying their expressions. Mr. Ord looked extremely tired, all thin, pale and drawn. Randy's death and Ruth's confession and suicide had almost done him in. But, she didn't want these people to raise her child. They had made such a mess of Randy and Ruth—how could she trust them to be able to help her raise this child? They would take over if she agreed to live with them. Carefully, weighing every word, Danielle replied, "I am sorry

Mr. and Mrs. Ord, but I have a nice place and I would really rather stay in my own home."

"Nonsense, we wouldn't hear of it," Mrs. Ord flushed.

"I am truly sorry, but my mind is made up. I will be sure that you get plenty of time to visit with your grandchild. I just can't live with you. I barely know you."

"We will have our lawyer speak with you after he has a chance to review this. I will have Randy's child living with me one way or another. You can't possibly give him the life he deserves. I'll see to it that he is taken away from you at birth unless you agree to live with us and let us give him all that he is entitled to."

Danielle set her jaw, determined not to let the Ord money make her a prisoner. "You go ahead and try if you think you can. I am not giving up my child. Please leave now. We have nothing further to discuss." She turned over in the bed with her back to them.

March found Danielle in tears when he arrived. She told him about the Ord's visit. "Don't you worry. I'll help you take care of these bills, and the little tyke. You don't need the Ord money," March said without thinking.

Danielle smiled weakly. "You would, too, wouldn't you?"

"You know I would." March answered. He pulled her to him and held her.

Meet Billie A. Williams

Billie A. Williams is an author of fiction, non-fiction and poetry. She has published non-fiction stories in Thema Magazine; Guide, a magazine for children; Novel Advice.com and articles, columns and features in newspapers such as Rhinelander Daily News, The Nicolet New Times, Minocqua Daily Herald in Wisconsin and Pine River Daily News in Colorado. Her short stories, Flash fiction, and poetry have appeared in Mystery Time, a Sister's in Crime publication, Word Mage.com, Great Write Shark.com, True Love Magazine and various anthologies. Her book reviews have appeared on Patricia Lewin, Story Lady, Writing Etc. and other web sites. She is a member of Wisconsin Regional Writers Association, National Association Of Women Writers (regional representative), Sister's in Crime and Women in the Arts Program. She lives with her husband in a small rural town in Northern Wisconsin where the winters are cold and long, but the people are warm and friendly

*VISIT OUR WEBSITE
FOR THE FULL INVENTORY
OF QUALITY BOOKS*:

http://www.wings-press.com

**Quality trade paperbacks and downloads
in multiple formats,
in genres ranging from light romantic
comedy to general fiction and horror.
Wings has something
for every reader's taste.
Visit the website, then bookmark it.
We add new titles each month!**